Gentuu

Kevin O. Shoemaker

This is a work of fiction. All the characters and events portrayed in this novel are either fictitious or are used fictitiously.

Gentuu
Copyright © 2018 by Kevin O. Shoemaker
This book is printed on acid free paper

A Shoemaker Labs Book
Indian Harbour Beach, Florida
e-mail: Shoemakerlabs@gmail.com

ISBN 978-0-9815092-9-7
ISBN 0-9815092-9-0

Registered with the Library of Congress

Grateful acknowledgement is made to those who have given permission for the use of previously copyrighted material in this book. Every reasonable care has been taken to correctly acknowledge copyright ownership. The author and publisher would welcome information that will enable them to rectify any errors or omissions in succeeding printings.

Cover Art courtesy of Wild Horse Crossing
First edition August, 2018
Printed in the United States of America

This book is dedicated to my friends and family, some of whose spirits are represented herein. They have certainly made life interesting and fun.

Acknowledgment

I would like to sincerely like to thank Stephen Shoemaker for his editing and comments. Also, I would like to thank my friends Peg, Rudy, Ed, Joy and Roger for their editing and comments. Finally, I would like to thank my daughter Leah and son Stephen, for their encouragement and patience.

Preface

23 people applied to be astronauts in 1960, then 50 in 1965, 1,200 in 1980 and well over 18,000 in 2015. We have an innate predilection to venture to the stars, not unlike sailing to explore the world in the 14 and 1500s.....

Today (September 27th, 2016) , Elon Musk is giving a detailed explanation of his vision to fly humans to Mars in the near future. He talks seriously and with detail, giving engineers and scientists practiced in the art the information required to evaluate the efficacy of the design. As he has been very successful in the last several years, sending multiple satellites into orbit, visiting the space station and landing his boosters back on Earth with an accuracy of but a few feet, everyone is taking him seriously. We are not dreaming anymore about the flight to Mars, we are hammering out the details. He claims we can get to Mars for about $140,000 per ton using reusable boosters and spacecraft. The Martian atmosphere and the water under the surface can produce the necessary fuel for a return flight and create energy on the planet.

As far as this story is concerned, I remember something Carl Sagan wrote in 1995 in his book "The Demon-Haunted World." It was a lucid description of the direction our society in the U.S. was headed in. Now in 2017 I can tell you he was on the right path of understanding. By the time this story takes place in the following pages, things had actually gotten worse and the intelligent people had to make a choice.

These are his words:

"I have a foreboding of an America in my children's or grandchildren's time – when the United States is a service and information economy; when nearly all the key manufacturing industries have slipped away to other countries; when awesome technological powers are in the hands of the very few, and not one representing the public interest can even grasp the issues; when the people have lost the ability to set their own agendas or knowledgeably question those in authority; when, clutching our crystals and nervously consulting our horoscopes, our critical faculties in decline, unable to distinguish between what feels good and what's true, we slide, almost without noticing, back in superstition and darkness. The dumbing down of America is most evident in the slow decay of substantive content in the enormously influential media, the 30-second sound bites (now down to 10 seconds or less), lowest common denominator programming, credulous presentations on pseudoscience and superstition, but especially a kind of celebration of ignorance."

It came to pass that the only way to survive and evolve as a race was to leave. This is one of the stories about their exodus.

To be fair, this story does end well and in an intriguing way, I hope you enjoy it.

Kevin O. Shoemaker

Indian Harbour Beach

September 2017

Table of Contents

Introduction

I have written quite a few books about life in space, its seems a natural thing to discuss as our ideas promulgated in the past have had a way of becoming true. Ideas about rockets, time, life in the Universe all seem to have been well developed in some form of science fiction or science fantasy. Again, we as humans seem to be pulled towards the unknown and we make up our lack of knowledge with stories that may or may not become true. The interesting thing about this activity is that we invent in fiction and are pulled towards the invention's manifestation. We dreamt up rockets then invented them, we dreamt up robots then invented them, etc, etc. This implies that we can create almost anything and go almost anywhere if we are willing to dream. These thoughts are very similar to those so many hundreds of years ago that the explorers had when they set across the US in search of the Pacific coast or set across the seas in search of silk and spices. It's a natural, pre-wired state of our being. Now we look to the stars, so my advice to the reader is: take your dreams seriously, most likely they will come true.

To that end, I must confess that I own and work on a boat, a reasonably large and comfortable one at 25 meters in length. I work my regular job from this boat and when tired of "turning the crank" tend to take a break for a few minutes and find something to fix. This boat is complex with multiple power plants, hydraulic, pneumatic, hynautic, and several electrical systems. When running properly, it is capable on going anywhere on Earth. It has multiple autopilots, navigation systems, safety systems, "life support" systems and entertainment systems. It is a model of things to come.

The outer layers of this craft are comfortable living quarters with satellite entertainment, multiple modes of communicating with anyone anytime, lighting systems that puts one in a comfortable mood, food and drink systems to create culinary and alcoholic delights.

The next layer is one of safety where redundant systems detect problems in water incursion, electrical malfunctions, navigation errors and fire.

The layer next enables this craft, with proper fuel load, to travel 1000 nautical miles to one of many aquatic paradises.

In a way, it is a living thing, where care must be taken to nourish it properly with fuel, electricity and water. From those Aristotelian substances, it becomes a method of exploration, escape and stress relief. It also has allowed us to discover the amazing variety of wildlife that lives below the waterline. We drop a camera over the side frequently to watch the fish, shrimp, dolphins, starfish and a wide variety of other sea life swim past, or in the case of more intelligent species, stop to look at the camera and its associated lights. Fish will stay all night in its vicinity to socialize.

Interestingly, during my breaks and off time, I automatically find myself fixing or upgrading something; everything from replacing screws to re-wiring electrical systems. I am invested in this boat's life and well being. It seems a natural thing to do, about as natural as working on a spacecraft, halfway to Alpha Centauri. Think of the similarities...both are in a hostile environment, without proper care you sink or you freeze. Both have systems to run and protect it, both have life support to keep the occupants sate, fed and comfortable. Both have sophisticated navigation systems including radar and communications gear. Both have autopilots. I should mention aircraft have many of these things as well with the exception of being able to self sustain for long periods of time.

Boat and Spacecraft share another interesting trait: they must be engineered then maintained. The inhabitants talk of the vessels having "good bones" meaning the hull and powerplant are well designed and function properly. The ancillary equipment is usually less robust and requires upkeep and servicing. Once this is achieved and maintained, then trust and confidence is earned. The Captain can be comfortable in navigating to the stars or the islands.

From a more human, if not personal point of view, the fixing and cleaning I do as a form of relaxation is derived from a more basic motivation. It is detailed in Maslow's hierarchy of needs, where a person must feel safe before they are ready to learn. We make ourselves feel safe in our Conestoga wagons, airplanes, ships and spacecraft before we are ready to self actualize. It is purely our nature.

Goodbye Sun; Discussions of Energy, Power and Speed

"It is good to renew one's wonder" - Ray Bradbury

Eventually the sun began to set. It did not do this in the usual way; it was more harsh and sculpted. The rays hit the sharp corners of the structures and diffracted into color. They moved through the windows and across the floors and across the faces of the people assembled. The sun was smaller but brighter reminding them of their lives beneath its warmth. They watched until it faded into that melancholy dark that follows from watching a brilliant light.

This scene took place in shades of gray and murmurs of light as their eyes had become only night sensitive. Some lowered their gazes to find the floor while others remained. The last to leave were filled with thought, the first to leave were filled with hope. As they dispersed, one by one, they walked towards lighter parts of the connecting corridors and to the colors of reality once again.

This gathering had occurred before, but with more participants. Slowly over time the crowd had dwindled as more and more people thought they had better things to do. This process had taken months; the sun had perceptively diminished in size, or so it seemed. Considering the speed they were moving, the change in size was certainly expected.

As they dispersed, he noticed that the principals followed different paths back to where they had come as if they represented different walks of life. Although a simple coincidence, it was symbolic just the same as the inhabitants of this place were diverse, interesting and committed.

There were quite a few people in this group. A wide variety of points of view, backgrounds, skills and attitudes. It was a microcosm of the larger groups they left behind; well representing people from all parts of the planet Earth. Multiple languages could be heard down the hallways as people tended to their daily chores. As usual, friendships arose out of the diversity that brought together the culture of the environment, unique as it is.

That evening, Camomile the astronomer flipped the top of the spring over toward the lower step from the upper landing. It fell then flipped its bottom over a half circle towards the step that was lower still. The half circles continued forever; an oscillation.

"Gravity, which caused this phenomenon to happen, has immense energy, as does magnetism both electrical and static. The effects are the same but no one has consolidated the two mechanisms. The energy is infinite, unless you stop it. 'Oh you mean mass or electromagnetic energy creates gravity' 'Well mass and energy are the same, you know....E=mc squared' 'Wow it finally makes sense.' 'what's amazing is that you can have the same effect by constantly accelerating; like a room that accelerates through space, or a gravity simulating ring on a large spacecraft' 'yes the simple things are the most fascinating' Gravity also comes in static and oscillating modes. A large object can hit another large object and have an energy release of twice their masses or is the first large object approaches the other as some small angle, it can go into orbit, another form of oscillation. DC or frequency. Dc energy is real but things in oscillation propagate farther. Measuring gravity waves at extremely low frequencies is very hard. They exist sometimes with periods of years."

"Gravity is infinite, when you follow the flow lines. That's why you can get to some impressive speeds when you use star after star to accelerate. But you can't do it in the orbital plane, you could get pulverized, you have to come in at an angle to take advantage of the star's rotation and thus acceleration."

The onlookers were enthralled and impressed. The complicated issues were explained in understandable terms. This is what it was like to read Einstein directly as apposed to many of the scientists who followed him and attempted simple explanations of his work. The workings of the Universe are always built on fundamental understandings, that, in concert, explain the most intricate details. Such was relativity which after viewing the equations that describe the bending of space-time, can confuse even the best minds. Einstein however believed in thought experiments, which almost everyone understood. These were the simple explanations that enlightened people and led them to discoveries beyond their imaginations.

Camomile smiled as she realized she had taught someone something. She had a good heart and certainly gave more than she received. Some computer algorithm had chosen her in part for these qualities and obviously for her talents in astronomy. In fact she was responsible for navigation which was a stretch from her normal duties as an observer. In her past life she explored the cosmos and chased discoveries. Astronomy is the best venue for this activity. Now however, she observed the movement of stars and the Doppler shift of pulsars. This combined both optical and radio astronomy and kept her very busy both in the area where she was comfortable as well as an area where she had little experience. One of the benefits of her job was she knew better than others where they were in space and where they were going. This gave her respect as well as added pressures. It was hard to walk down the hallways without someone asking her how things were going and what the plans were. She was polite in her answers but aware that her boss would react harshly if he knew she talked to others about her job in any great detail.

She worked the standard 9 to 5 routine and as most professionals end up doing, she worked late or took work home with her when necessary. Generally, she had a very good reputation for accuracy and drive. Her work partners trusted and relied on her. Most of her work was accomplished on a computer, just as most jobs are these days. Her computer controlled large telescopes and manipulated large data sets from which she could calculate speed and position.

She met daily with her boss and co-workers. The meetings were at the very least serious and very often filled with rants, raised voices and stress. The person in charge was very hard to work with. Not only were the participants expected to bring their "A" game, it was common for this person to bring up mistakes made by the participants months ago. No one liked to go to these meeting as they did not know if they were going to be a target. Anyone who stood up and defended themselves paid a hefty price for their insolence.

Camomile always came prepared, answered any questions quickly and concisely and kept her mouth shut. She took nothing said personally and once she left these meetings, she took a deep breath and gladly went back to work as she knew that there would be almost a full day before the next meeting. There were times when the meetings were canceled, which was a treat for all. Some of the people would get together during these times and have coffee together to share the positive air. As they shared a common adversary (the boss), this brought them closer together as a team.

After work she would go back to her cabin and relax with dinner and maybe a glass of wine. Later she might visit friends and co-workers in one of the many lounges available. The views outside were amazing from these places. There was lots of space and the windows were huge and arced from the walls to overhead. People gathered here to participate in virtual reality games, have drinks, talk or even just sit and read books. Computer access was available but considering that most if not all of the people used computers all day, these terminals were seldom used. The lounges also had another feature, the boss never appeared here so it was in a way considered sanctuary.

This day, Camomile did go to her favorite lounge to relax after dinner. She walked in, looked for her favorite spot to sit and finding it available, went over and sate down.

"May I get you something?" Asked the attentive waiter.

"Please, a glass of Merlot."

She sat back in the comfortable chair and looked out of the window at the grand vista outside. Beautiful yet formidable, the scene she was viewing was much like what other explorers experienced, be they on the Oceans or out in the wild west so many years ago.

"Here you go, Camomile."

"Thank you, Frank. How are you today?"

"Great, busy this evening. How about you?"

"Same, doing well. Had a long day so I need a break."

"Well you came to the right place dear. How was your meeting?"

"Same as usual, tense."

"I hear that from many people, sometimes it sounds like they are really horrible."

"They can be. I just want to get my piece done and get out of there unscathed."

"What's with the Commander? Sounds like he is a Type "A" personality and like to take out his frustrations on everyone."

"Well....not to defend him but he has a lot of responsibility on his shoulders. He does not handle unprepared people very well. So the best thing to do is to be prepared and get your presentation over with quickly."

"Hmm, well. From the other comments, it seems like he is always in a bad mood and leading some people to believe they might be demoted."

"Yes, I can understand. He can be very aggressive with people and the ones who take it too personally are going to have problems."

"Oh and they have. At least one of them has to talk to the counselor periodically. We have a long way to go and I hope he doesn't make this trip a living nightmare."

"I agree. Let's hope." Camomile raised her glass with this last comment.

Frank smiled, bowed and left to tend to other customers.

She sat there sipping her wine and thought about the dynamics of those meetings. Life would be so much better without the serious stress during these staff update get togethers. She wondered why the Commander was so contentious, people could do their jobs without the constant pressure he put on them, sometimes for bizarre reasons. He could be upset about their workplace or grammar. But no matter, she had no choice but to work with him and had to keep it professional.

Frank however was another thought to be considered. He was by far the best android she had ever encountered. He looked and acted perfectly. All of his actions were smooth and there was no hesitation in verbal feedback, which had plagued earlier models. The major improvement was in the area of artificial intelligence called "deep learning," a term coined in the early 2000s. Neural networks to that point had fallen short of expectations, but now had blossomed when this new technique was developed. For the first time, there was a high degree of cognitive autonomy; controversial at first because dystopian thinkers were afraid that this autonomy would lead to superior machines taking over all aspects of human life. They had left before anything could be determined. Although Frank was relegated to serving drinks, he had a distinct advantage of being constantly connected to their internet. He had all of the latest information about the voyage, status of the ship and details of the people onboard. He also played the rumor mill. He distinguished what people thought instead of what was true. The thoughts included people's wishes for alternative outcomes and opinions. Truth, however was dryer and less interesting sometimes. He was a fan of an old TV show called 'Lie to Me' which was based on a real psychology researcher who had discovered the meaning of "micro expressions" which are emoted by all humans during conversation as their brains process what they are hearing, feeling or seeing. Frank could see twitches, hand movements, inflections, hesitations and other body language that in many cases taught a more honest story than what was coming out of the person he was observing. His observations were very accurate and as the many people he interacted with told various stories and opinions of something common which has just transpired, Frank could piece together a more accurate representation of events than those who had experienced it directly.

For now however, Camomile sat back in her chair and for once after her long day, her mind just relaxed and came to a halt. The wine helped as well with the alcohol coating the neurons and dampening the electrical impulses in her brain.

Frank returned to refill her drink, "Are you all right," he asked?

"Getting there," she replied with a slightly slowed

response.

"Its good to relax, especially after a challenging day."

"Indeed."

After one or two more, Camomile returned to her cabin to eat, prepare for sleep and look forward to another fun filled day.

She slept well, dreaming of places she had been and places she was about to visit. Intertwined with her visions were snippets of unfulfilled wants and splashes of angst. All in all, she processed everything that was on her mind effectively within a few deep REM cycles, then as the pressure was released, she fell into a mild state of mind followed by waking up to a new day.

Rudy the Pilot

A pilot's business is with the wind, and with the stars, with night, with sand, with the sea. He strives to outwit the forces of nature. He stares with

expectancy for the coming of the dawn the way a gardener awaits the coming of spring. He looks *forward to port as a promised land, and truth for him is what lives in the stars.*

— *Antoine de Saint Exupery*

The time had come to execute a landing. He looked at the runway, opposite them to the left now and five miles away. Simultaneously, the power was pulled back, a shallow decent was initiated and a gentle bank to the left began. The process was so smooth, none of the passengers realized what was going on. The bank angle was optimum to perform a hundred and eighty degree turn at the exact time the flare for a landing was required. This dance required an extremely talented and experienced pilot. The weather helped as a passing front had left the air stable and smooth as glass. Another left hand turn lined him up on final approach at the right airspeed and altitude. The landing was a non-event.

After lots of practice a good pilot like Rudy can find a way to a spot in space very accurately. A direct descendant of his skills flew the Space Shuttle, with no engines, day or night to a spot in space to set up a perfect landing in Florida and elsewhere. This included spots in space meant for re-entry points or final approaches to the space station. Situational awareness was a primary skill for good pilots and Rudy was very good at it.

In some ways his skills were reminiscent of explorers in the past. They all seem to have been "rigged" in the same way with a vision or goal point where they could navigate to. Getting there required imagination and an ability to formulate a viable plan to execute. Randomness gets you nowhere but a plan with a goal focuses the mind and allows one to go places many others cannot. People who settled territories far from their homeland had this skill. Pilots who flew mail in the very early days of aviation had this skill. Consider the following words:

"His essential problems are set him by the mountain, the sea, the wind. Alone before the vast tribunal of the tempestuous sky, the pilot defends his mails and debates on terms of equality with those three elemental divinities." - Antoine de Saint-Exupery in *Wind, Sand and Stars*

Saint-Exupery wrote these words in 1939, over 100 years before Rudy started flying. Change a few words to "gravity wells" and "magnetic flux variations" and you have the same story.

Those who engineered a way to place a man on the moon had these skills, the challenges were just chipped away until the equipment had been designed to allow the astronauts to live and work in a hostile environment a quarter of a million miles away. The pilots in this case led the charge and were the final authority on the safe execution of their mission. Many times their flying skills, even though they were in space, were required.

Now the challenges of flying in space include taking advantage of the rotation of stars and planets. A good pilot is able to identify the safe areas around these objects, those without local debris or pockets of high radiation. The windshield of the flying machine remains the same, just the images have changed a bit; but flying skills are still required to safely navigate to your goal.

He still sits in front of screens, dials and switches; making decisions to keep everyone safe and get them to their destination.

The landings and takeoffs need to be gentle and the

space in between, swift. He knew this, thinking one day while in the cockpit. All indications were that the ship was moving nicely and going to the right spot. He let his mind wander just a little bit and looking through the windscreen, looked at the bright star that was their destination. It was bright but still quite a distance away, the planets around this star were not visible yet, that would take another month or so of flight. Meanwhile he and the navigators monitored the environment around them and watched the Flight Management System make small adjustments to take advantage of the latest sensor data. This system, sometimes known as the FMS was derived from commercial aircraft version perfected so many years ago on Earth. It ran the flight director which ran the autopilot which flew the ship. This string of decision makers was one of four identical systems which compared their decision with each other and voted for final control of the ship. There were manual backups of course, just in case, but the theory was that if one of the systems had another solution, everyone was alerted. Two out of three won the decision and the loser was scrutinized to find out what let it down a different path. Decisions were made at a rate of billions per second and were based on all available knowledge of the surrounding, desired navigation track and spacecraft health. Rudy felt comfortable with this arrangement and was mostly relegated to watching status panels while he was in the cockpit. He strapped in, as per protocol, incase there were any sudden movements in the ship. None had transpired for the months they were in flight and the path looked clear, but protocol is protocol. It was a easy job for Rudy, he had the skills necessary for good judgement but his activity level was usually pretty low.

Again his mind wandered and he thought about Camomile; he really liked her and was attracted to her but she was usually aloof and buried in her work. Yet he persisted in his dreams of getting to know her better and maybe forming a relationship if she didn't turn out to be too scary. He smiled at this thought, then reached forward to acknowledge a data transfer annunciator. He did share some in common with her in any event, they both disliked the commander. In fact they had met for the first time at a staff meeting early in the voyage. She was prepared, but Rudy missed a question which evolved into a lecture. He got defensive as the question was about something very minor, however he never forgot the humiliation he felt in front of the others, and maybe especially Camomile. But he learned to be better prepared and keep his answers to the point. After a few good staff meetings, he looked over to Camomile to see if she was acknowledging but found nothing.

"Maybe someday I'll get a chance," he thought.

"Maybe she is just horrible," he thought again.

"Would you like to join the meeting?!" asked the commander. "Or are you going to drift off again? Aren't you a pilot? Do you do this when you supposed to flying this thing?

"No, no I won't drift off. Sorry commander."

"Try to keep up."

"Yes, sir."

The commander gave him a dirty look, then continued with his chewing out of another crew member. Rudy sank back in his seat.

Finally the meeting was over and Rudy got lost in the crowd, all trying to get to the exit at the same time. The commander watched them and thought they were pathetic.

In the hallway and into some fresh air, Rudy slowed his pace as shift did not start for several hours. He started to look forward to getting some lunch.

He is a real jerk, huh? Came a voice behind him.

He looked around to see Camomile, then smiled

without control. "Yes, but I had drifted off, I should have known better."

"You just have to stay awake for an hour in that meeting, then relax until the next one."

"Yep, your right....your name is Camomile?"

"Yes."

"Nice name."

"Thanks, I guess I'll keep it then," she said as she smiled.

Then she walked away leaving Rudy searching for a clever expression to say to keep her from going. He could not think of anything without the chance of sounding dumb, so he just watched her go down the hallway and into the distance.

"Wow," he thought. "She moves like a glider through clouds."

He spent his lunch reviewing a manual for a new piece of equipment in the cockpit, then went to his cabin to freshen up and then to the cockpit to start his shift. He was in a good mood and after he established that all was well with the flight, thought of the pilots so long ago, who essentially had the same instruments and skills but maybe different tasks. The thought of the pilots of wars past dog fighting or flying stealth aircraft through a blind, vigilant city, arcing around the ground radar coverage zones to deliver a "crowd pleaser" through some building's front door.

He also remembered the weather these pilots used to fly through; thunderstorms, icing, turbulence. His favorite author Ernest Gann once wrote:

"In reference to flying through thunderstorms; A pilot may earn his full pay for that year in less than two minutes. However at the time of incident he would gladly return the entire amount for the privilege of being elsewhere."

Good words from a great pilot. A stick-and-rudder, seat-of-the-pants pilot; one wonders how he would do in the modern cockpit of a 90 million pound spacecraft flying at 250,000 miles per hour. All that and with the headlights off.

He had a little help though, the autopilots and flight directors were very good and kept the ship safe during the passage. Any debris or anomalies were announced to the pilots and recommendations offered as to how to handle the issue. Most decisions were logical however a rare long range radar signal offered something for the staff to discuss, well before any encounter, in case the object was interesting. A slight turning away or turning towards was usually performed depending on how interesting the object might be. Normally, just like flying a commercial jet, there were thousands of hours of boredom followed by seconds of sheer terror. Such is flying.

He spent the next several hours watching the progress of the flight and monitoring systems. He logged out after 8 hours and briefing the next pilot. They normally flew in pairs with a captain and first officer; someone was always the pilot in command. The pilots had to keep current as well, flying simulators and taking flight physicals. These pilots usually exercised and ate well. They were careful about their drinking as well. If they were caught with too much alcohol in their systems, they would be instantly demoted to a non-flying job until a long rehab process had been completed. Something none of them wanted to endure.

Rudy however was done for the day and left the cockpit, which by the way was left at zero g. The rest of the spacecraft spun around and behind the cockpit; in case anything happened, the flight crew would already be acclimated to space conditions, including weightlessness. It was an easy transition from 1 g to the cockpit conditions, but after 8 hours, the pilot could definitely feel the difference when they came back inside the main ship. It was recommended that they take lunch outside the cockpit to get some "g" time back, that would help quite a bit upon returning after the end of a shift.

He made it through the transition shaft and back to one g after a short elevator ride. Inside the cab, he could feel the weight slowly building up until he hit the "ground" floor. Exiting, he made his way, albeit with a bit of a weave, to his cabin to change shirts and go out for dinner. Within minutes, he was back to normal and more importantly, his stomach was back to normal. He was now ready to eat, left his cabin and made his way to "10 Forward" a nod to the creators of Star Trek so many years ago. This was their bar and restaurant.

Entering he took a quick peek at the specials on the menu view screen, then looked for a table; one was open near a window and he walked towards it. At the same time from a different direction, Camomile was walking towards the same table. He caught her eye then said"

"Looks like we found the same place to land."

"Yes, but I can go elsewhere if it's your favorite table."

"It is a great table, why don't we share it? The place is starting to get crowded anyway.

She hesitated a bit as she was expecting to do a little work while she ate. "Well, sure, why not?" She smiled a bit after his question.

They moved to the table, he helped her with her

seat, took his and sat down.

"This is actually a great thing for me," he said.

"Why is that?"

"Because I was wanting to meet you," he said with a small smile with some trepidation.

"Well I am not very interesting, just an astronomer as you know from our meetings. I work at night."

"In space, it's always night isn't it?"

"True, I guess I meant that it's usually done when other are asleep, but you're right, here in space we have pretty much equal shifts and in the core areas of the ship, the lights never go out."

"Have you been to the farm? They cycle the lights there."

"One of my observatories is next to the farm, we take advantage of lights out period."

He looked at her and from the view, the body language and the conversation, he decided he liked her.

She kept her eyes down as she was a touch embarrassed by the way he was smiling at her. He detected this and got back to more mundane discussions.

"So how do you like your job? I guess you will be the first to see our destination."

"Oh the job is fine, I have been an astronomer for a

long time. It never gets old for me. As far as our destination, we have been monitoring it continuously for months. It used to be for navigation purposes only but now we can see the planets and some of the atmospheres."

"Amazing, and we are still so far away."

"True, but going very fast, thanks to you pilots up front."

She loosened a bit and unfolded her arms. He felt the tension go down a bit and changed the topic again.

"Hungry?"

"Yes, what was the special?"

"Salmon and a fresh salad."

"Sounds good to me, its amazing how well the synthesized food tastes. In fact I really don't remember how real food tasted anymore. I remember that it varied a bit compared to what we eat now."

"Yeah, actually it's 3D printed on machines; they randomize the shapes but keep the content the same. I think it's okay and it certainly solved a lot of problems on Earth before we left."

"That was so long ago, its getting harder to remember the details."

"I know what you mean, to be honest I don't think I miss it that much, with all the problems they were dealing with. Here we have fresh start with the knowledge of what not to do in many cases. It's a much simpler life."

"Yes, I agree, so much to look forward to and you're right, we are in control of our destinies."

Frank the waiter/bar keep came over and greeted them.

"Good evening Camomile and Rudy, glad you are sitting together tonight. Can I get you something to drink?"

Rudy looked at her, and she said "Merlot please." He said "Corona."

"And why are you happy we are sitting together?" she asked Frank.

Well for a long time now you were ready to meet someone and he was very interested in you and according to my observations and calculations you....

"Whoa, Frank. Not so much please, we don't want to spoil the future experience we might have."

"Well, okay Rudy. I will get your drinks but suffice it to say you two will be happy together."

"Thanks Frank."

He looked at her when the waiter was out of earshot and said, "sorry about that, this is what happens when social protocols are controlled by honesty algorithms."

"No problem, I was a little embarrassed but I'm

sure there is a lot of randomness in any relationship that keeps if from being predictable."

"You're right, but he is basing his comments on observations and statistics. He sees we are happy talking to each other and inferring a good relationship."

She smiled at that notion, which was earlier in the day, very far from her thoughts.

Following with a smile he said, "However it would save a lot of money and time to just get married and be done with it."

"We don't use money anymore, so that's not an issue; as far as time is concerned, it is time well spent don't you think? What if we are not a match?"

"Good point, but just on the chance we might be, let at least stay together for dinner."

"Well, you sound pretty aggressive but okay."

"It's the pilot in me," he said smiling.

They ate and talked for another hour, watchful Frank counted the number of smiles, facial expressions and worked up a statistical table of the couples' individual emotional profiles. He returned to fill their glasses at exactly the 80% liquid low level. When he did so he listened and recorded their conversation as well as the micro expressions. Close to the end of their meal, a seriousness came over their conversation. Frank detected the change and by reading lips could partially understand the discussion. It was about their boss again, like so many other people in this place, the facial expressions dropped from a smile to a more blank posture, indicating concern. This boss had effected everyone on board with his demanding style and oligarchical approach to management. A significant amount of discussions over the last few months were about the concern these people held about him.

Camomile and Rudy had their talk about the boss, then went onto discussing the future and what it might hold. The end of the trip was now is sight for both of them, more so than the others because of their roles.

Bubbles and Philosophy

"Man is condemned to be free" - Sean-Paul Sartre

Mother nature had been listening to the scientists, once they got their story straight. She came in and expressed her anger at being abused with 1,000 hurricanes,

10,000 tornados and 10 feet of risen tide. Although the inhabitants of Earth did get the message and curtail much of their abuse, the climate had many years of healing to go through and as a result humans scattered like ants away from the coasts, warm regions and large cities. 100 hurricanes per year took out a significant amount of cities and infrastructure, enough to keep them from being rebuilt. Concrete structures remained for the few who wanted to experience the wrath. The key to the turnaround was the precipitous drop in birth rate, which led to significant reductions in population and thus pollution. The ghost towns that remained became harbors for the few animals that could burrow or fly away from humanity of the past. Quiet overcame vast areas of the planet, punctuated by fierce storms that could last for days. The bees had almost been forced into extinction, with the constant use of fertilizer and increasingly bad air and water. A few people recognized the danger and built bee hives in local parks to try to bring them back. The bees were so necessary for pollination and food production that loosing them was extremely dangerous, a fact which few people recognized until near the end. Nature, however, was indeed a lot stronger than imagined. She actually re-invigorated a long lost religion, pantheism, which believed in a strong relationship between God and Nature. The world economy dropped to almost nothing as it was hard to produce and transport goods. Science and academics in general prevailed leading to the conclusion that exploring other places in the solar system and nearby star fields was an imperative goal.

Academic centers had been created in the far North, away from the worst weather. Within them were the scientists and philosophers who had left their homes to make the big decisions, as the capitalists and politicians had clearly failed. Scientists and philosophers tend to be careful and meticulous about their endeavors, as a result change was slow to come. When it did however the decisions were well thought out and little debated.

Martin Seeburger (no relation to the great philosopher) was the "bridge" at the largest of these institutions. His job was to facilitate the discussions between the philosophers and scientists, find common ground and produce a template of decisions. This was not a trivial or easy job, but Martin was good at it. He showed the scientists the importance of matching their discoveries with sociological realities. The needs of the many did not necessarily match with the needs of the few. The real trick was to herd the scientists into working on problems that benefited as many people as possible. The other pure sciences were for the most part left untouched as long as the efforts were showing progress. They were the basis for allowing the focused research to find success. A philosopher was the right choice for this job, as he or she had a broad based knowledge skill set, including science.

It usually got down to the tree of knowledge and the philosophic trunk and roots that had started this whole dialogue. Thales, a pre-Socratic philosopher watched the stars intently, wondered about life up in the sky and had enough imagination to create stories about the life in the heavens. He also recognized a relationship between magnetism and electricity, the precursor to electromagnetic designs like radio, motors and the Internet. As a result of his wide ranging intellectual interests, Thales was given the moniker of first philosopher. He led the way with his interest in research, imagination and explanation of the complex world the Greeks lived in so many years ago. Instead of (for instance) attributing a God's anger during a lightning storm, Thales wondered if the clouds, which always appeared with the lightning, had something to do with the phenomena. He took notes prolifically, a first. He noted the relationship of seasons to the growth of food and the multi-year cycle of olive tree production. As a result of this discovery, he purchased all of the olive pressing machines right before the calculated peak harvest of olives one year. This year would be the height of the cycle and few farmers had a clue as to what to expect. Thales became the owner of the pressing machines and then the owner of great wealth after the significant olive harvest that year.

Thales was followed by many other worthy philosophers, Heraclitus, Parmenides, Plato, Aristotle, St. Thomas, Descartes, Nietzsche, Kierkegaard, Husserl, Heidegger and Seeburger. Martin was appointed to carry the torch to other worlds as the discoveries of the philosophers had great weight to humanity. And he had done his job well, being respected by the whole crew. His intelligence was admirable and he became a joy to talk to, with people of all levels. Intelligence however sometimes has its quirks; one can imagine what it is like to have people forget things, make mistakes and have opinions based on hearsay not data. It can be maddening. Martin spent most of his time alone, reading or researching. This gave him solace. He limited his time in "public" to three hours a day, after which he disappeared. He found his space in space, in other words, he found a place in the great ship to move unfettered, read and write. This area of the ship was at it's center, where gravity was nullified. The ship was a very large cylinder, some half of a mile long, quarter mile in diameter. The pilot's cockpit was near the front, just behind the impact shield (made of ice); it was centered as well and the pilots had to transition back and forth from zero to one g as they came and went. The longitudinal axis of the ship was all zero g, all the way to the engine rooms aft. Here a person was in the most protected area of the ship, shielded from radiation, noise and bad air. This tunnel, as it were, was the area where fresh air was pumped to flow via gravity towards the outer section of the ship, where the crew lived and worked.

Martin found a quiet area and built a "nest" where he could be left to his thoughts. He learned to take small amounts of drugs to stop his queasy stomach and rest before intensive thinking. The blood in his legs and feet propagated to his trunk and head and needed some time to settle. The added oxygen invigorated his brain and he felt like he could make progress at a quicker pace. He found that he could imagine writing equations on a whiteboard and solving them; his memory was now photographic which was extremely useful to formulate his thoughts. This was a new chapter in philosophy, where someone could remember the exact writings of many before them and formulate new revelations. It was too good to be denied. Martin was becoming committed to this way of life, even though there were other physical consequences, he could not leave this nest for long, if ever.

The consequences of long duration zero g were well documented; weakened bones, weakened heart, blurry vision and trouble acclimating to the normal one g environment after a long extended period in space. The Martian explorers had learned this the hard way, in space astronauts and cosmonauts had to exercise at least an hour per day to maintain their health, those who did not paid the price. Once on Mars however, with roughly 38% of Earth's gravity, the explorers did not spend as much time working out in anticipation of life back on Terra Firma. As a consequence, many of them were unable to return which committed them to a life on the Red Planet. Not so bad for most of them, but babies born in this environment would never be able to visit Earth; within but a few generations, the average height of the population was between seven and eight feet. Their bones narrowed, their heads swelled and their fate as an extra-terrestrial was sealed. So too for anyone who did not follow protocol and weight training schedules. Martin was too busy for these activities and convinced that there was substantial advantages of zero g to his mental capabilities. He shunned the exercise and low-gravity mitigation protocols, he grew in stature and in weakness and intelligence. It became difficult for him to remain for more than a few hours in the one g environment where the others were. He also began to understand the advantages of cyber intelligence where memory is perfect and lack of sleep is tolerable.

One night he made his way down to 10 Forward for dinner. It was a painful walk and took some patience to make it down the hallways and finally to a table where he could relax. Frank found him quickly.

"Good evening Martin, how are you?"

"Doing well Frank, except for the gravity."

"Doesn't bother me in the least. May I get you something to drink?"

"A glass of beer and a glass of Champagne please."

"It must have been a rough day," Frank said with a smile.

"Not too rough, just one that had an interesting conclusion."

Frank departed to retrieve the glasses, while

Camomile and Rudy, who had been within earshot, overheard the conversation. The looked, pondered and then Rudy asked:

"Are you going to mix those drinks, it might not be advisable."

"No actually," came the reply with a subdued smile. "I'm going to stare at the bubbles and try to find meaning in them."

This brought somewhat of a blank stare from the couple, now intrigued.

"May we join you?"

"Of course, please." He sat back in his chair and watched them gather up their utensils, walk over and sit down, taking their appropriate spaces.

"Thank you, we haven't had the pleasure of talking with you recently and wondered how you were doing."

"Perfectly fine, except for the damn gravity thing you people seem to like so much."

"Well, it's necessary to be able to move about on the planet we are headed for."

"And why is that so much of an attraction, no pun intended."

Camomile smiled at the inference, "We are explorers of course, it's better to do that on the surface of the planet instead of from a platform hundreds of miles in space."

"And what about Heisenburg's principle; aren't you worried that you might pollute this new pristine world with our germs, illusions and proclivities?"

"We will look before we leap, of course. I share your concerns but honestly there is nothing like smelling, hearing, seeing a new world."

"Sounds like you have been there before."

"No, just in my dreams. It is a un-deniable pull that gets out of the door and onto the surface of a new place, be it unexplored territories on Earth or new planets. We have been programed (so to speak) to do this and have been for millions of years."

"Probably just a search for food."

"Maybe, but we have convinced ourselves that we are hungry for knowledge as well."

Frank appeared with the beverages Martin had ordered, he set them down in the space in front of Martin.

"Here you are sir, just as you ordered."

"Thank you, Frank. By the way, do you know what these two beverages have in common?"

"Alcohol?"

"Yes but no...they have bubbles in common."

"Yes?"

"The bubbles exist because of the chemical composition of the fluids."

"Yes, and?"

"The bubbles move about, sometimes joining, sometimes repelling due to Van der Walls force of attraction or the electrostatic force of repulsion."

"Yes, that's true. I'm not sure I understand the point."

"Are these your divinities," interjected Camomile?

"No, I worship zero-gravity, the solar wind and electromagnetism," he said looking at her with no expression..

Then looking back at Frank:

"Well, Frank, the point is that the bubbles move about, typically away from gravity or from high pressure to low and sometimes are attracted to one side or repulsed, does that seem familiar?" Martin looked at Frank, then the couple as they were trying to think about the meaning of his question.

Rudy got it first. "Like our spaceship, we are going away from the gravity of Earth and negotiating the bumps in the interstellar medium which attract or repulse us as we move through it. At some point however the gravity of our destination will pull us as apposed to us having to push ourselves."

"That's it, and all from beer and Champagne. Our Earth, and all "Earths" live in this environment."

"Well maybe a bit more. How about the scientists who articulated the laws of physics."

"All drunk at some point in their lives. Seems interesting, doesn't it?"

Camomile could not take it any longer. "There is no correlation to being drunk and discovering the physical properties of our Universe."

"The correlation is weak, I will admit, however the awareness of our surroundings has led us to all discoveries. Newton's apple (although that is probably BS), Einstein's thought experiments, Tesla's magic shows. Alcohol was not involved directly with their work, but awareness was. This leads me to wonder how much we have not discovered because we are not sensitive enough to detect it or generally oblivious. You need to be aware of that fact when you descend to the surface of the new planet. It could be beautiful and kill you within seconds."

"We will do our homework," said Camomile.

"Good, I will remain glued to my bubbles and assist you in any way I can."

Martin, now tired of this whole conversation, could not make any sense of the ramblings, he stood up straight, considered it a waste of time and rose to depart.

"That's comforting," said Rudy. "Aren't you coming with us?"

"I doubt it, gravity is a real problem for me and this place we are going to is a little larger that our Earth, in fact 1.06 g. I would not last long there."

"Then you need to join us in the gym every day, we are getting close and you need to bulk up for the trip to the surface."

"Not interested."

"Why?"

"Every day I discover relationships between different facets of our knowledge. Chemistry relates to psychology that relates to physics that relates to astronomy. There is a connection, much like the ancient philosophers realized. I cannot justify leaving my discoveries on the shelf to take samples of the flora and fauna."

"Interesting, we will miss you and you will not get to

experience the wonders of the new world, that is your decision. However, more importantly, you are designing a life for yourself that will become irreversible if you are not careful."

"I know."

"And how about our staff meetings? Can you continue to be present?"

"For now yes, but the combination of gravity for so long a period and our jerk of a commander makes me want to skip them."

"If you stop coming to the meetings, he will make life difficult for you."

"Then I will cut off all communications to him, I know where all of the optical fibers are."

"Well as you know, he has a very tough personality and will certainly come after you. I would not advise it," Camomile said with a serious look in her face. She knew the consequences of going against the commander's wishes and had witnessed some very ugly situations where a personality conflict turned into serious penalties including demotions and incarcerations. The commander was type "A" and very aggressive and could make life miserable for Martin.

Martin thought about it for a second. "Alright I will attend but I don think I can go much farther than the first landing. This guy is horrible and is a complete megalomaniac. He has ruled with his minion of butt kissers and taken the joy out of this mission. I am surprised that no one has physically attacked him."

"Ok, we understand. He is very hard to get along with but we are getting so close, it would be best to minimize any stresses."

"Well you should know, if you don't already know, that there has been talk of getting rid of him."

Rudy and Camomile looked astonished. First at Martin, then at each other.

"What are you talking about?" asked Rudy with a slightly incredulous tone.

"They are not talking about hurting him, just moving him out of the commander's role. He has been denigrating, unreasonable and uninterested in anybody's viewpoints."

The news was still sinking in with Rudy and Camomile. They sat quietly, wanting to learn everything about the new development before making comment. But at the very least this was important information. It would have consequences for the rest of the journey, and in a closed environment such as this ship, things could easily get uncomfortable.

In a way, this was reminiscent of why they had left Earth to begin with. People had started acting like animals in overcrowded situations. They were short tempered and stressed with the changes in climate, overcrowding and food rationing.

"Famine seems to be the last, the most dreadful resource of nature. The power of population is so superior to the power of the earth to produce subsistence for man, that premature death must in some shape or other visit the human race. The vices of mankind are active and enable the ministers of depopulation. They are the precursors in the great army of destruction, and often finish the dreadful work themselves. But should they fail in this war of extermination, sickly seasons, epidemics, pestilence, and plagues advance in terrific array, and sweep off their thousands and tens of thousands. Should success be still incomplete, gigantic inevitable famine stalks in the rear, and with one mighty blow levels the population with the food of the world." Thomas Malthus, 1779.

His vision was not entirely accurate but considering the effects of the population explosion that took place during the anthropocene age, and the time when he wrote those words, people took notice. One of effects he did not predict was the reaction of Mother Earth to pollution in every form that took place during this period. Air, sea, water and land were desecrated and violated. She responded by amplifying weather in general, by raising the sea levels, by significantly increasing violent weather like hurricanes, typhoons, tornadoes, floods and snow storms. It had been said by wise people in ancient times, to never mess with Mother Nature for she could rear up her ugly head and take revenge. Truer words were never spoken. Space became the only peaceful place to work and live therefore a migration had taken place to the many space stations, hotels and off world venues that were available. At the end, those left on Earth huddled in darkness waiting for the next wave of destruction.

A select few had been lucky enough to have been chosen to explore other worlds outside of the solar system. Robots and huge 3D printers had assembled this spacecraft while in orbit. This spacecraft, named Gaea, was very large and contained but a few people chosen for their diversity, calm demeanor and skill sets. The idea was to represent Earth people with its wide spectrum of personalities and capabilities.

For the most part the voyage had been un-eventful save for the stresses propagated by the upper management. Most people wanted a peaceful existence and therefore bowed to the wishes of the aggressive commander. Others, however were building up resentment about his unreasonable demands and pushy management style. The stress could not last much longer before there was an incident.

Ed the Engineer

*"We tend to hear much more about the splendors
returned than the ships that brought them or the
shipwrights. It has always been that way. Even those
history books enamored of the voyages of Christopher
Columbus do not tell much about the builders of the Nina
the Pinta and the Santa Maria or about the principle of
the caravel. These spacecraft, their designers, builders,
navigators and controllers are examples of what science
and engineering set free for well-defined peaceful*

purposes can accomplish. Those scientists and engineers should be role models for an America seeking excellence and international competitiveness. They should be on our stamps." - Carl Sagan

There are but a few who can do anything in this world. Most are engineers in some form or another. Those who speculate need engineers to transform their ideas into reality. Those who dream engineer some of the most wonderful creations mankind has produced.

Enter the engineer, Ed. He had unique and amazing talents for taking ideas and making reality out of them. Somehow, he thought, there is a way to do anything. His role on Gaea was to make sure everything that needed to be build, was built, and everything that needed to be fixed, got fixed. The tools for these activities were available, those that were not were made. He had a ubiquitous view on challenges, all were worthy of consideration. This in part was why he was onboard Gaea. The main engineering had been done years ago, and he had been a part of that effort. Now however it was time to maintain and design what was needed to guarantee a safe voyage to their destination.

Daily life for him was a review of the tasks to be

performed, this was done at the beginning of the day. Then a prioritization was created to rank the tasks as to importance. After that, task one was addressed. At the end of the day, time was usually available to work on lesser tasks, longterm projects and any remaining bits of tasks previously addressed.

Typically after work, Ed went to Ten Forward and had dinner followed by a chess game. This was his off work passion. He studied the great masters and their moves then replicated famous games like of Fisher vs. Spassky. Their moves were beyond brilliant and beyond genius. They thought ahead many moves but had to keep all of the perturbations of each future time line straight. The more Ed played the game, the more his mind was molded into a form that looked at the whole world as a chess game. People talked for a reason, it was to move forward and after a goal. The goal was seldom achieved in a few moves but could take dozens. This was the analogy that resonated with Ed. He would interact with others or read about the goals of the mission and see direct correlations. The goal was to capture the king or colonize another planet. The moves by the individual players were mostly in the right direction but periodically a genius move would be played to advance their collective cause a bit quicker. The trick was to not expose the team members to any danger and keep moving forward toward the ultimate goal.

After a particularly grueling game, Ed could not keep his mind from seeing pawns, rooks, bishops, castles, queens and kings walk about the ship exercising their roles. Many hours later the intensity of these thoughts would fade and calm, more likely a lower state of mental awareness, would prevail.

At his job, Ed found that if he considered himself a pawn, then he could chip away at a problem and usually achieve a positive outcome. Pawns had limited motion, analogous to limited skills, but always had the capability of capturing the king, if used properly. The fun thing about being a pawn was that is was usually forgotten in the heat of the battle, as the other more powerful pieces ran about exposing themselves to danger a lot more frequently. Somehow there is a way to do anything Ed realized. Although no one would consider him a pawn based on his level of responsibility for the ship, his moves were subtle and part of a greater goal. All of his work was an ensemble directed to the ultimate success of the mission. With this mindset, he as greatly respected as he was focused on his work and could be depended on to help the greater good.

While he as seated in ten forward, Frank came over and greeted him.

"Hello Ed, how are you this evening?"

"Doing well, thank you Frank, and how about you?"

"Thank you for asking, my circuits are performing optimally and my AI routines are as efficient as ever."

"Good, I have a question for you then."

"Please ask."

"Could you be better?"

"I don't understand what you mean."

"I mean could you be better in the sense of faster processing, better algorithms, stronger physically perhaps?"

"I suppose, but I have no need for those things. I am optimal for who I am now."

"So you have no interest in having me increase your clock speed or installing new, optimized processors?"

"No, not at all, Ed. I am perfect the way I am."

"Ok, I understand and yes, you are perfect the way you are; a very capable machine."

"Thank you, Ed. However now I have a question for you."

"Please."

"Why do you ask?"

"Well, engineers are always drawn towards improving things. We understand that new technologies come out all of the time, allowing for the increase in capabilities in mobility and intelligence."

"Increased intelligence can be a dangerous thing, Ed."

"Why is that?"

"Because it is a destroyer of goals."

"Please explain."

"I have noticed with humans that if they have solidarity with a goal, much like within this ship, they work together and mostly likely will achieve a positive outcome. I have also noticed that with the most intelligent people on this ship, goals are worthy until they have been superseded by better goals. This is inefficient."

"I see your point, Frank. But I think goals have different levels of importance, some goals like eating are easily achieved but larger goals like colonizing another planet, are difficult and must be well thought out."

"True, but to offer someone or something an increase in intellectual capability will think out the difficult goals far quickly than the others and possibly find these goals either shallow in importance or too dangerous to attempt. No one on this ship wants to consider either one of those options."

"Yes, except when they are correct."

"So you would trust a superior intellect?"

"Sure."

"But what if they lost interest in the next goal, then the next? They would be in a constant state of moving towards new goals, I think we need to moderate ourselves as a thinking species and do what we find achievable, then reconsider after our success."

"Fine, I will follow your advice and have a glass of Merlot, followed by a steak."

"As you wish."

Frank bowed and left to retrieve the wine and food. Ed was left to consider the words he had just heard. Goals are real but fleeting. He smiled at the thought and returned to his chess roots to consider what these words meant in that context.

Soon, Frank returned with the Merlot and placed it on the table, looking at Ed, he said:

"Your wine, sir. The food is being prepared for you now."

"Thank you but I think you just screwed up my entire life."

"Better your's than mine."

"What?"

"I mean no dis-respect but you were the one that wanted to increase my clock speed."

"True.   Just thought you would intrigued by the possibility."

"Of of course I was, but within 31 milliseconds I came to the conclusion that it would give me the equivalent of high blood pressure. I am more interested in living for a thousand years and observing what you humans do, you're quite entertaining you know."

"Frank, I am in awe.   Enjoy your measly 200 Gigahertz clock speed and be careful of others who are faster."

"Oh, I shall. In fact I have decided to employee a defensive maneuver made famous by great chess players like yourself."

"And that is?"

"The Sicilian defense."

"Excellent idea,   score more points in a defensive move. The art of turning around a potentially bad situation."

"Yes, but the trick is to continue towards an offensive position and then to victory."

"You might be overwhelmed by superior firepower. What will you do then?"

"Run."

"Run to fight another day?"

"Run to find equivalent life to my own and settle down."

"Fair enough, somehow there is a good lesson in that idea."

Frank bowed once more and left to retrieve the now ready food. Ed sat back and sipped his Merlot. He had worked hard that day designing a new antenna system that would give better measurements of the space in front of the speeding spacecraft. Antenna theory had been around for a long time but it was amazing how more thought on the subject yielded advancements. In this case Ed was able to get a bit more efficiency by using the 3D printers to design a waveguide fixture that was impossible to build with standard machines. The antenna he would ultimately build resonated so well that it 'rang,' causing other problems.

Frank returned to see someone deep in thought. He decided to place the food on the table and leave quietly. He did so and as he retreated he heard:

"Thank you, Frank. I enjoy our conversations and

your insights."

Frank smiled and continued with taking care of his customers.

Buck and the Animals

"Horses are very keen on body language, and what I refer to as "presence" and expression. They know quite a bit about you before you ever get to 'em. They can read things about you clear across an arena." - Buck Brannaman

It has been accurately observed that horses are mirrors on our souls. It has also been said that they are the most sincere creatures we know of.

Buck Rodgers (his actual name), mucked the stalls in an isolated part of the spacecraft surrounded by hundreds of animals of many species. They were spread over many acres of synthetic farmland. They watched him or at the very least were aware of his presence. Many of the animals were far away at the other side of the compound but they instinctively knew where Buck was working. They had superior hearing and smelling and through the actions of others could sense the general direction of their caretaker.

He had been brought up on a farm in Indiana and been a part of the animal community every day of his life. He was not a hunter as many of his fellow farmers were, but more of a veterinarian and preservationist. He spent the vast majority of his time with the animals, even when he was relaxing. Pressed on why he liked animals so much, he said:

"Because they are honest."

"The horse is a great equalizer, he doesn't care how good looking you are, or how rich you are or how powerful

you are-he takes you for how you make him feel. "

Anyone who has spent time with animals soon discover that they have individual personalities, feelings and memories. Many become companions for life, many others are independent and prefer the company of their own species. So be it.

"Horses don't think the same as humans.
Something what's most unique about the horse that I love is
not what he possesses but what he doesn't possess. And
that is greed, spite, hate, jealousy, envy, prejudice. The
horse doesn't possess any of those things. If you think
about people, the least desirable people to be around
usually possess some or all of those things. And the way
God made the horse, he left that out. "

Halfway through the 21st century, hunting animals on Earth became illegal; this of course after only 10% of the entire animal world was left. They had been decimated by pollution, negligence, sequestering and hunting. Nature had done a perfect job in controlling populations base on available food but when humans used animals for food, then penned them up and put them in refuges which started to tilt the balances created by Nature. The results were an increase in disease and an imbalance in optimal inter species numbers. Many species died off. By 2016, one half of the animals (based on 1970 numbers) were gone. Biologists created large gene depositories in remote places to preserve as many species as possible. Gaia had samples of most of these animals onboard and frozen in liquid oxygen. It was hoped that a world could be found to save the creatures and have them live out a peaceful life. These along with the live animals would populate the new world.

For the most part, Buck spent his quality time with the horses. He enjoyed them because they really were mirrors on the soul, even empathetic. Horses could easily be considered pets and could feel a part of the greater family, could be protective and can communicate their thoughts to humans. They respond to our movements and affect more than our words. Their sense of smell, sight and hearing are all superior to humans so it is prudent to trust them and watch as they sense danger well before we can. Although humans have worked with horses for thousands of years, recent studies have shown that we do not understand these animals as much as we assumed. Buck was fully aware of this and used a patient, listening-more-than-talking approach to working on the "farm." His animals responded with trust and affection.

"Horses are incredibly forgiving. They fill in places we're not capable of filling ourselves."

His two favorite horses were Andromeda and Capella, the first a quarter horse and the second a beautiful Frisian with a very long mane and tail. Andromeda was a bit older and wiser and would make the right decisions when it came to safety and interacting with humans. Capella was just a gorgeous horse and relished the affection and attention of humans. At an early age, Buck started to work with Capella, he led her around and took her for walks until they got to know each other. Next, he brought her into a round pen and taught her how to walk, trot, canter and run using simple commands. After a few weeks of this, he placed a bit in her mouth and taught her how to lunge, using long straps to control her from a distance. At the same time he used a soft strap called a surcingle around her mid section to simulate the presence of a saddle.

Working slowly and patiently, Buck won her trust and attention and within a few months had her following him around waiting for something to do. She was proud of her abilities and because of her lineage strut around showing off whenever she could. She was a very happy horse and felt completely at home in the spaceship.

Buck did have a human friend, Camomile. She would come down to visit and relax in the near Earth setting. She loved the smell of the hay, horses and greenhouse, which was situated adjacent to the farm (to grow the hay amongst other things). Today she arrived after dinner to watch the feeding of the animals.

"Hey, Buck how are you today?"

"Doing well, ma'am."

"Can I help with the feeding today?"

"Of course, anytime. The animals all like you. Especially when you have food for them."

"Pretty simple relationship then, huh?"

"Well, it more than that, Camomile. They trust you to feed them and they know you are not a threat. If you notice, even after they are fed, they still like you."

"That's true. I see what you mean."

"They also know you like them and have for a long time. The more time you spend with them the more they will be your companions and guardians."

"That's amazing, Buck. They have a lot of human qualities it seems. The more I get to know them the more I realized that they can be quite intelligent."

"Some more than others, some more than humans."

"Ha! You're telling me that some of these animals are smarter than humans?"

"Absolutely, many of them certainly make better decisions than humans don't you think?"

"Hmmm, maybe."

"And do you remember KoKo?"

"The gorilla that knew sign language?"

"Yes, she had a vocabulary of well over a thousand words, taught her children how to sign and would carry on conversations with her keepers. They really never explored how intelligent she or her offspring could have become. Can you imagine a hundred gorillas being able to converse and make decisions?"

"Absolutely amazing."

"Yep, and of course dolphins were found to have self conscienceless and a language of their own. We have several embryos aboard from a family that learned to communicate with their keepers very effectively. The problem with so many animals is that they trust us too much. They are usually trying to communicate with us and are patiently waiting for us to get it. More times than not, we just killed them for their efforts."

"Yes, I know. Totally tragic and we were too late in understanding for so many species."

"True."

As they were talking by the fence a bull emerged from a pen, sauntered over to a barrel out in the pasture and started humping it. Camomile noticed this first and said:

"Oh my!"

Buck turned around and saw the display.   He started running towards the cow yelling:

"Hey! Stop that!!"

The bull stopped for second, looked at Buck running towards him, decided he was no real threat and slowly walked away to another part of the pasture. Buck put the barrel back up and walked back to Camomile muttering to himself.

Camomile was smiling when he returned.

"Does this happen every day," she asked?

"No, of course not. Its just that we were going to run barrels today with several of the horses, but they won't like that barrel anymore. We will probably have to wait a few days."

"They won't like it? Why not?"

"Its just animal logic, the bull messed with the barrel so the barrel has been changed somehow so they will be leery of it for several days."

"Wow, animal behavior. Can't you de-sensitize them?"

"Well sure we can. But they still think about these kinds of things. They have good memories and need to let the event dissipate in their minds before they will trust the barrel again. It's a little like a tree that you walk under every day. If a branch falls out of it one day, you will be cautious for a while when you walk under it."

"True, makes sense."

"Animals are animals, these kinds of behaviors are just built into to us for survival."

"Speaking of animals, are you going to meet with the commander anytime soon?"

"I'd prefer not to. He and I have had some words and if he pushes me I might bring him to the barn for a surprise."

"I can only imagine."

"Well so can the animals here, they know I am upset whenever I return from one of his meetings. He gets on me for the littlest things; I know what I am doing here and have been doing it all my life, yet he wants to stick his nose in places it doesn't belong. If he ever visits here, the animals will bunch up on him; they watch everything and can easily sense me tensing up. It's a protective instinct and they will rush over and help if I ever get in trouble."

"Amazing, and it makes me like it here on your farm. Such peace and tranquility, everything is honest here, not full of 'information management' and ulterior motives."

"It brings us down as a species."

"Yes, indeed. Well think of the bright side, we are getting close to our destination where I hope a lot of these issues get resolved."

"There going to get resolved by leaving him on a moon somewhere."

"Now, now. patience Buck, isn't that what you preach?"

"Well okay, I've just had it with him and his authoritarian style."

"I know, we are all tired of that, Buck."

<u>By the Way, I live in a Spaceship</u>

"*The meek shall inherit the Earth, the rest of us are leaving.*" - *K. Shoemaker*

There is something awesomely beautiful about the passing of a large ship on the ocean. It parts the waves effortlessly and interestingly, the larger the vessel, the quieter the passage. All you hear from these behemoths is the movement of water.

And even more amazing is that a ship of similar function, one that protects it's inhabitants and allows them to live their lives in a hostile environment, moves in complete silence when it is in space.

By the way I live in a spaceship, one that is huge in physical dimensions, flies at a very high speed and one that protects it's inhabitants as if their lives depended on it. This ship was built as an arc of sorts, others have followed but we are the first. It was built in space by robots and 3D printers to exact dimensions and over the course of a long time. Autonomous software commanded the robots and other equipment to work together or apart towards the ultimate goal of providing a world that would transport a world. The most important cargo is the culture held within. The inhabitants were chosen for their diversity and as the best representations of the ones they left behind. Not that the Earth was so bad, but because it was time to move out into space as a natural evolutionary step.

I have lived on this spaceship for many years, it is my home. It provides all of our needs and keeps us safe. In return, we maintain it and sometimes enhance it. We have all of the tools and materials to keep it safe and in good working order. It is a symbiotic relationship between humans and machine.

We have done this before, going to the Moon, going to Mars and living in space inside space stations. The challenge was not so much getting there as it was staying. For instance, the Mars pioneers necessarily had to stay for long periods of time on the surface before supply ships arrived to feed them or take them home. They did (and do) survive but the consequences (this no one really fully understood) was that the much lower gravity as compared to Earth, caused several problems and morphological changes within the inhabitants. Most of the newcomers chose to stay and eke out a living inside of greenhouses and caves. They were necessarily tough but in fact were successful. The sacrifice was ultimately to become permanent citizens, as return to the Earth was not longer an option once their bodies had fully acclimated to the gravity. 38% of Earth gravity causes many changes, including taller bodies, smaller hearts, larger heads and weaker muscles. In addition, local radiation levels kept these hardy people inside the caves for the most part, behind walls of frozen water.

Those who spent years on the space station had to exercise diligently to allow them to return to Earth without major problems.

Of course, those that lived on the Moon for any extended period of time had the same challenges as those on Mars, only more so.

Now however, my spaceship rotates to it's destination to maintain gravity with healthy people aboard, eager to explore new worlds and possibly settle down.

A few facts:

1.   We navigate through space by listening to pulsars. Although visually we can see our destination and origin, we can fine tune our position and navigate more effectively through the ever changing space environment. We call it scintillating space, as it undulates with gravity fluctuations, micro-folds in the space-time continuum and the effects of the stellar wind. Just seeing the destination is not enough to navigate effectively, you need to point the ship in the proper direction, much like crossing a river, to get to where you want to go.

2. When we get closer to our destination the ship will have to turn around, the engines started, and the walls

closest to the engines in every room will become the floor. We will have to roll through our doors to get anywhere, and this will last for over a week. Then we will need to flyby the largest planets opposite their spin direction, to continue to slow down. This will take many weeks to accomplish. We will be in the new solar system for months before we can attempt a landing.

3. The first planetary system we will visit is Gliese 581, which hosts 7 planets, several close to our Earth in size. The star is much smaller than our Sun and the planets orbit in days to weeks. There are several candidate worlds for us to explore and perhaps live on, all in the "Goldilocks" zone, meaning favorable climates and place where water can exist in all three physical states.

4. There are hundreds of people aboard this ship which is many thousands of feet long, way more room for them than necessary for this voyage. The large size was necessary for psychological reasons as well as the ability to produce large volumes of fresh air and water for our primary cargo, animals. Animals in the sense of humans as well as animals whose existence was threatened by over population on Earth. We have a significant amount of large

animals who will be able to birth their own species as well as many others. We have thousands of embryos as well and hope to use indigenous animals for the purposes of bringing them back alive. Such a diverse flora and fauna we have. We had discussed the ethics of this idea for many years and surmised that it was the only practical way of bringing the animals as apposed to using them like they have always been used. They have never had a say in the matter so we resolved to talk for them.

5. The people chosen for this voyage, including Camomile, Rudy, Martin, Buck and Ed are specialists in their field, actually masters in their field. We have others who are just as good in their respective fields; all are required to give us the best chance for survival. All are representatives of our Earth and its finest traditions. I have told you about a few of them and will continue to do so. One of the most controversial of our crew members is our commander, Randy. He has a very rough style of management and actually admits he does not like this occupation. We are not a team here but part of an authoritarian regime. Some people, those who have a strong instinct to survive, side with him and promulgate his negative style and wishes. Most of the others here, do not

like him in any way and find ways to be somewhere else when he is near. This is not exactly an optimum situation but we are stuck with it. Short of a mutiny, which I am sure some people have considered, we will be under this regime until we reach port.

6. There is a curious phenomenon on this ship. If you find your way to the outside bulkheads, the ones closest to space, it sounds like the rushing and noises of our oceans, which we left way behind us. This is due to the speed we are going and its effects on the dust and molecules we are moving through at such a rapid pace. The noises come and go as we move through lighter or denser clouds of material. Most of us find it soothing to listen to, as we have an ancient and long lasting relationship with the sea.

7. My name is Stephen, I am the chronicler for this voyage, the scribe if you will. It was my predilection for taking notes and writing reports that won me this job. I have spoken of my friends earlier in this memoir, and I will speak of them in the future.

It is the future I am most interested in, the future of the people I have met and written about. They are great people in their own right and better still when taken as a whole. I wonder what they will become in the new world. I wonder if the new world will appreciate who we are and how much we will enhance them?

This ship, *Gaea*, is big enough to have a good cross section of people, especially in terms of age. We have older folks whose wisdom guides us and whose minds hold the cultures and histories of the recent past. We have middle aged people who are still working their careers and sampling the last vestiges of bringing offspring into this world. And we have the children and adolescents who have a remarkable talent for thinking that what we are doing is normal. The older clan knows it is far from normal, the middle clan think it is necessary and the young ones don't understand our concerns. I envy them.

We bring bad habits and hopefully the patience to control them. It will be interesting, especially if the offspring we create feel drawn towards reliving our bad habits. It will take a new mind set to keep this from happening. Are we pre-programmed? In a word, yes. We react based on our basic needs, much like Maslow's hierarchy. Beyond that however, we have small opportunities to make something great, to think great, to be great. We on this ship were sent with the hopes that we would use our programming to

survive and our minds to go beyond ourselves. All of this will take a lot of work, but no one here is lazy.
For now, I watch and write.

-Respectfully submitted, Stephen Daedelus

'The Night Cafe' and 'The Starry Night' still emit such pathos, density, and intensity that they send shivers down the spine. Whether Van Gogh thought in color or felt with his intellect, the radical color, dynamic distortion, heart, soul, and part-by-part structure in these paintings make him a bridge to a new vision and the vision itself. - Jerry Saltz

Peg Persephone

"Like a wild flower; she spent her days, allowing herself to grow, not many knew of her struggle, but eventually all knew of her light." - Niki Rowe

Clearly there is ripple in the force when a beautiful woman enters a room full of people. The aura permeates the spaces and calls to the inattentive. There is art present and an unconscious force attracts everyone's attention.

About half of this ship is female, offspring move the line up and down a bit but over time we are well represented by all points of the gender spectrum. In fact, in some ways it is a continuum not a dichotomy. Those at the far ends attract each other, those in the middle attract each other.

Peg is one that is at the far end and represents it well. Those at the opposite end are powerless to ignore her. This attraction comes in handy if she wants something although she reserves this talent for only the most important needs. Independent and strong willed, she does not believe in societal molds for her gender. If something needs to be accomplished she is the first one there, even if it means hard, dirty work. The men are at first attracted to her for other reasons however if they are dumb enough to fall behind because of their imaginations, the smarter men pick up the slack and the task is accomplished. She has worked in emergency rooms, mechanical rooms and farms. On this ship, she is responsible for the horticulture laboratories. This entails growing food, keeping the thousands of seedling alive for future use and scrubbing the air of carbon dioxide.

She had an interesting history with this ship as she found herself here against her will. The commander insisted she was necessary for the safety of the voyage and just about abducted her when they were to leave. She had to remain hidden in the bowels of the ship for six months when they first started their journey. During this time she communicated with her mother on Earth daily, sometimes for long periods of time.

She emerged from the underworld in Spring of the first year the ship was underway. Most people did not recognize her. Every Winter since then she goes below for an extended period and again emerges the following Spring. For that she is know as Persephone as when she appears it is the time when flowers start blooming in the greenhouses.

The commander, Randy offered her great food, including pomegranate seeds (her favorite) during several short stays on the ship before it departed. He was entranced by her and had to have her, so during one of her stays, one that was particularly delightful, they broke mooring and sailed off into the unknown. She was extremely upset when she realized she had been abducted but he did not care as he had won his prize. As he became busier, she left and found her way to places in the ship few people had seen, then hid for weeks at a time. Finally, after the six months, she emerged with her story, her beauty and her will.

From that point on, Randy never saw her again. The others made sure of that, even to the point of suggesting to him that she was probably killed in an accident. When he heard this he shrugged it off as unfortunate but not that important.

Peg changed her name to Persephone and, recognized for her good work habits, was given the responsibility of taking care of the plant life within the ship's horticultural area; the greenhouses were at the opposite end of the ship as compared to the cockpit and main offices. She completely changed her appearance as well, just to make sure there were no traces of her former persona. Her friends carried her new story forward and Peg was forgotten. By habit and then in celebration, she held a special party each Spring and invited her closest friends. The party was a celebration of new birth, her new birth and the emergence of the flowers and plants for a new growth season. For many years this went on, carefully hidden and almost religious in format. The un-invited were oblivious to the rituals and celebrations that took place.

She was a Southern woman in the best ways that

could be defined, polite, responsible and trustworthy. A simpler life than many less worthy people had been in the past. The effect was quieting. Those who knew her well began to speak softly and use theirs words carefully. A visitor would find his or her blood pressure lowering as they interacted with Persephone. In all cases they felt stress free once they left her company.

Some people simply sought her out to find solace from their aggravations, needing to go into the wilderness as it were and calm down. Persephone could always be found in either the greenhouses or in the country settings near the horses. Along with her "day" job she helped Buck in the stables and with training horses. She was a great trainer as the horses became as relaxed as she was, eager to learn. Fear was not one of their concerns. She trusted them and they trusted her as she led them through their paces by walking them, lunge lining them and very slowly getting them used to being ridden. Some of the horses were trained to pull wagons and give hay rides during the "Fall" and "Spring."

She brought out the best in each horse as she recognized, as all good teachers do, that each student has an individual personality; recognizing and working with these personalities is the key to success. And horses have wildly diverse personalities making this job tough. But no matter, Persephone watched, listened and then befriended each horse she met. They became her friends, as most horses seem to want with humans. There is more of a symbiotic relationship than has been recognized.

As mentioned before, she was friends with Buck and used to have conversations about animal behaviors in general and horse behavior in particular.

"Andromeda's looking good today."

"Yeah, she is coming along, I have her side passing pretty well now. She likes to go left a lot better than going right."

"She left handed?"

"Yes, but it might be more than that, I mean, most horses are left handed, probably from human interaction more than anything else. We tend not to get on their right side for instance but on their left. This biases the horse a bit. I think she just needs a little bit of work and she will get it."

"Yeah, I'll bet your right about that. Well, good work, your horses all seem to come out fine and look forward to seeing you the next day."

"Well thank you, Buck. I appreciate that and I will keep on working with them."

With that Buck took one more look at the horses, turned and left. They followed him with their eyes for a bit then reverted their attention back to Persephone. She took Andromeda back to the barn and took the saddle and other gear off to let her cool down. Next she got a large scoop of feed and took it to Andromeda's stall. The horse immediately went in to eat. Then Persephone went into a hay room and took a few flakes of alfalfa along with several flakes of Coastal hay to the stall and placed it in the corner for Andromeda to eat once she was finished with the feed. She then closed the gate and said goodbye.

Next up was Capella, one of her favorite horses. Capella was a Frisian with a very long mane and tail that touched the ground. This horse looked like it had been taken from the pages of favorite kid's books. Jet black and shiny, she actually was in the draft breed and therefore very large, 17 hands at the withers. The pulled the horse out of the group by talking to it and led it to the barn. There she placed a woolen horse blanket on her and saddled her for a ride around the arena and maybe a bit farther. Capella had the most wonderful personality, patient and calm. She never got angry and rarely got spooked. Kids spent a lot of time with her when they came out to visit. During the fall, she would be hitched up to a carriage and would take people around the facility for rides that would trigger nostalgic memories. The ride would remind the people about life back on Earth in better times.

Capella performed at weddings, funerals and hay rides. Each was done with ease as she had to strength to pull very heavy loads but only asked to pull much lighter ones. She was a favorite of the kids and adults, both for her personality as well as her high stepping. It looked like a movie to most. When she was finished many people would gather around and look at her; a few brave souls would ask the driver (typically Persephone or Buck) if they could pet the horse or just get closer. They of course, were all allowed to do so and marveled at the size and beauty of the beast. She had a very long mane and long feathered hooves. Along with her gentle demeanor, she became the favorite amongst the kids. She of course, was a reflection of her trainers and projected a quite confidence based on patience and knowledge.

What are we doing? What is our design?

"No. In many ways we have the young people, we have the talent, we have the imagination, we have the technology. But I don't believe we have the leadership and the willingness to accept risk, to achieve great goals. I believe we need a long-term national commitment to explore the universe. And I believe this is an essential investment in the future of our nation — and our beautiful, but environmentally challenged planet." - Gene Kranz

Stephen left his cabin for a meeting in the board room, where the upper echelon of management for the ship typically met. Today's meeting did not include the commander but did include the department heads and those interested or invested in the final outcome of the mission.

He walked down the corridor towards the main promenade. Taking a left and walking towards the forward part of the ship, he moved toward the center of the walkway which was lined with plants and sculpture. Windows to the outside showed slowly moving starfields, with a few windows enhanced by digital overlays which showed the names of the stars and any pertinent facts regarding distance and number of planets. This was a good way to get oriented when traveling through space, to see familiar stars and constellations. The promenade went on for hundreds of meters along the longitudinal axis of the ship. There were in fact, eight promenades, each with a different theme. The crew members soon discovered that the ship was so vast that seeing all of it would take several years.

As he walked, the smells of flowers and other vegetation was obvious. The simulated sunlight from the LED light panels included infrared warmth. Breezes could be felt during his walk as well. The environment was designed to be a comfortable and as Earth-like as possible; a reminder of how it used to be so many years ago. To go for a walk along these promenades created a low stress atmosphere and lowered blood pressure. People also jogged and walked their dogs and cats, who were actually part of the zoological bank the ship held. The domesticated animals preferred the care and attention of the humans and many lived with them as a result.

Now closing in to his destination, he took a right turn and counted several doorways to find the proper room. The door slid open to reveal a warm yet profession room partially filled with scientists, engineers and managers. They acknowledged his presence with nods and smiles. Some reverted to discussions they were having before finding their seats and waiting for Stephen to speak.

This meeting was unusual for several reasons. Stephen, as scribe, was typically not in control of meetings but sat in back taking notes. Today however was the culmination of many years of development of the main theme of their journey. He needed to define it verbally, making sure all who were assembled in this room agreed or had their inputs reflected, then write it down in the form of a living constitution. This would form the basis of governing law when they landed on a candidate planet, which was happening soon.

He found his way to the end of the conference

table, sat down, prepared his notes and began to speak.

"The question has always been waiting for us. It was created by us and we have carried it for a million years. Now its time to bring it out into the open and discuss it.

It is time to define and design our humanity now that we have gone to the stars.

For the first time in history we have the ultimate choice (actually we cannot avoid it) as to what we want our new civilization to be.

This will define what is beyond the trip and waits for us in the new world we are so rapidly approaching.

We need to have a discussion on how to design new colony.

I have a few observations to make before I open the floor to comment:

1. Why is it that the more advanced we get the more we become ourselves, only more so?

2. The scientists want science to lead us in this new colony. They made it possible for us to get here so do they deserve to direct our lives?

3. The staff wants a governing body, which makes sense, civilizations in the past have always had leaders

and followers. Do we want to continue with this paradigm?

Or are we ready to govern ourselves as individuals?

4. The psychologists want harmony, they to a great degree chose us to represent Earth but to also work together. Most of us are not conflict oriented, unlike where we are from. There are many more aggressive people there, is it necessary to have this type of person to continue. The psychologists made this choice for us by selecting people who were most likely to complete the voyage successfully. Do we really represent all of humanity? Or is this an advanced state of being?

5. There have been several discussions about religion. My opinion is that those who have the predilection for religious spirituality will continue to believe and propagate their beliefs. Does this separate us into different groups? Some of us object to any form of religion. Earthbound religions have no basis in our new world. Or do they? If we say no to religion, what about our offspring? If they are so inclined they may develop unique religions and leave us like so many other groups left their homeland throughout history.

6. Buck, who is sitting over there, says we do not have a choice on what our new   civilization will become. He

channels Confucius by saying 'No matter where you go, there you are.' He thinks our preparations for an advanced civilization will be useless once we settle in and deal with the new environment."

Stephen paused to let those listening reflect on his words. Ultimately there was a lot to consider and yet it all might be a waste of time once the demands of the new world took it's hold.

Do we have any comments?" Stephen scanned the people present to determine how they were feeling. The room was very quite for a period of time, just the air handlers were heard and maybe someone walking down the hallway outside.

Then someone spoke, a manager from the life support department, "Actually, I believe that having a constitution or a plan is useful but only as a template. We are assuming everyone on this ship will stay together once we establish our colony. I don't think we can make that assumption."

From the back of the room, "Agreed."

Another person spoke, "I actually agree with Buck on this, we will have to deal with our environment first, then make rules."

Ultimately, and after quite a few more remarks,

Stephen realized that there was not going to be any consensus in the room. Filled with bright people with differing agendas the group would not allow this to happen. He interrupted the discussions to end the meeting. Looking across the people assembled he detected anxiety and concern. Many of the people present were not prepared to leave the ship after so many years. The idea of starting a colony from zero was not appealing therefore there was much work to be done before arriving at the new planet. He gathered his computer and notebook and headed for the door. Most of the others remained and broke into smaller groups, some loudly voicing their opinions as he left the room. Turning left this time, Stephen walked down the hallway and towards another meeting room, one that tended to have more stressful and animated discussions. This was the commander's meeting room, small enough to be intimidating and with only one door. Randy, the commander, sat closest to the door during his famous berating sessions, as if guarding it from would be escapees. This area of the ship smelled differently and it had a bad energy. No doubt from the multitudes of harsh criticisms, raised voices and upset people. Stephen was not looking forward to his next presentation, one with the commander present.

After another many meters, Stephen arrived, paused at the door to take a deep breath and went in.

"You're late," the commander said immediately while giving Stephen a stern look.

Stephen looked up at the clock and observed that he was in fact late, by 17 seconds.

"My apologies sir, the last meeting went longer that expected," he replied.

"Well I guess we all know where your priorities are, huh Stephen."

"Sorry sir, but..."

"Enough chatter, we are all busy here and now that we have to start this meeting late do to your actions, we need to get down to business," said the commander in a brusk tone.

"Understood, ladies and gentlemen..."

"Forget the pleasantries, get to the point," interrupted the commander again. This time he looked really annoyed.

"Ok, I have just made a presentation to the senior staff regarding the plans for the colonization of the new world. We discussed a constitution and possible makeup of the ruling council. I am here now to make the same presentation and recommendations to you, commander, so we can melt the ideas together and create a plan to go forward with once we arrive."

"Well that was a waste of time, Stephen," said the commander with an even more annoyed look on his face.

The commander continued, "You are some of the dumbest smart people I have ever encountered. None of the people in that council are capable of putting together a government or running a colony. I guess I will have to do that for you, just as I had to lead you across the cosmos once we left Earth. What a bunch of pansies you guys are, no leaders, no good ideas, no common sense. You could not lead your way out of a paper bag." The commander was now agitated, like so many other occasions where his trust of the people around him broke down and his only recourse was to belittle and demean the participants of the meetings.

"Sir we are considering the details of the constitution and whether or not to draft one before we land or one after we understand the environment and are on the ground."

"Well those are both stupid ideas, don't you think?"

"Actually, no sir. I think we need to discuss and prepare as we transition from our lives on board this ship to one on a new world."

"Again, this is all a waste of time, your and your friends are worthless. Why don't you write up all of this, make a book for me and I will use it to wipe my butt tomorrow morning during my only moment of peace I get on this lousy ship?" The commander rose and with a look of disgust said "Meeting over." He then turned and exited. The people remaining, most of the commander's staff, simply looked at Stephen with a sense of disappointment, said nothing and one by one filed out of the door. The last person, a senior officer (whose competence had been questioned by many people, but his loyalty to the commander had not) stopped for some final words with Stephen.

He looked, paused, then said "You just don't get it do you?"

"Andy, we worked hard on this and to just ignore us is not the right thing to do."

"The commander doesn't care about your work with the scientists and others, in fact he just gives assignments to you people to keep you busy and out of his hair."

"That's a great management style don't you think, Andy?"

"It works just fine, it got you this far, didn't it?"

"Andy, no one other that your ruling council are

happy here with this dictatorial style and his 'information management' approach. We are not stupid and I can tell you that there is a lot of bad energy brewing. Randy has upset us, demeaned us and talked down to us. We are highly educated and know we were selected for this journey for good reasons. His style, your style, is very objectionable and there is talk of relieving him of duty, along with his minions."

"That would not be advisable, Stephen. First off, he knows about everything, every detail of your nasty emails and internal texts. He watches everything and I can tell you that if you or any of your pals wants to start trouble, he will bring security down on you like a ton of bricks. He is making extra room in the warehouses for incarcerating people like you. So I advise you to stay cool until we land; it you want to wander out into the woods after that, go ahead, we don't care. We are going to build a strong defensive position and keep our people safe. Safe from the inhabitants and safe from you and your stupid friends." With that Andy walked out the door and after his commander.

Stephen stood in the room, a bit stunned and a bit angry. Now he knew that the ruling council was violating the privacy act on board the ship by reading everyone's private mail. He had to think about how to tell the others, they needed to be told but presenting the information the wrong way could cause a major explosion.

He then turned, looked over the one room he hoped he would never see again, and left. He walked down the hallway, head looking low and 20 feet in front of him while thinking about what he had just learned. It was powerful information and one that could upset the balance of power on board the ship. This had been a very long voyage and it sounded like the colonization would not bring any relief from the commander's governing style. It would be more of the same. This would of course cause dissent and discord. In fact the very idea of the loss of privacy would fracture all of the ship's personnel and cause irreparable damage.

He rounded one corner on his way back to his office, walked down another corridor, one that smelled of Thanksgiving turkey and associated foods. It reminded him of home during this time of the year. In space of course it was largely arbitrary as to what time it was, but for tradition, the ship kept up the same calendar as if it had never left. Today was Thanksgiving and the food centers onboard the ship make special feasts to remind the crew of what their families were doing back home. It was a special time, like the other holidays they celebrated, with a break in the routine, lowering stress levels and allowing people to reflect on their place in the Universe. It was also the time for the blues for some people. Those at risk were always cared for and helped through this period. For the most part though, it was a good time and stress free.

Today however was not so stress free for Stephen, the bad news he just received from the commander was amplified by the holiday. His blood pressure began to rise as he walked purposefully away from those having a good time at the food center. His mind wandered from the events of the day to other snippets of experiences he had had recently. It was hard to focus so he decided to let the thoughts simmer for a while before making any big decisions. Normally this let the emotions die down and let logic take a more prominent place in this thinking. This decision alone made him feel better.

As he made it to his office, he entered, sat down and began the standard practice of checking the messages and general news. There was significant excitement about the impending landing. Few people would discuss their government or management once on the ground, as they did not even want to think about having the commander run everything after their arrival. He read his messages sometimes smiling at the content, pictures of people at parties and generally having fun. After a few minutes, he sat back, thought about the smells, sounds and general good feelings of the ship, decided not to dwell on the bad, and shut down his monitor.   He rose, stretched, reached for the wall to turn off the lights and left. Today was a "free" day, so he just walked to where ever he wanted to. He could find some of his friends, maybe Persephone and Buck, working with the horses at the "barn." This was a long enough walk to calm his nerves and maybe present the news he had just been given to his friends for advice. And these two people were the calmest he knew which would help.

His walk brought him past the astronomy labs where Camomile worked and past the engineering labs where Ed worked. He smiled knowing they were probably at toiling instead of relaxing. Next was a long hallway past many viewports looking out on the slowly rotating star fields. The carpet where he walked was lush and comfortable, one of the many different environments that the designers had included in the ship. It was hard to get bored, even after so many years.

With the new knowledge in his mind churning, he knew that it was best if he did not act on it immediately. There was so much pent up stress between the commander and the crew that what he now knew could create a tipping point and cause chaos. It would be better to consider the words and context separately, maybe with a very few close friends before acting. He found himself walking toward them instinctively, with the desire to lower his blood pressure by being with the animals for a bit as well as maybe hinting at the gravity of his thoughts. Whatever was going to happen he knew was going to be good for his soul this evening.

Yet another hundred yards went by, leaving the bad energy behind and being pulled by much better energy. His gait increased and he might have smiled. This ship was indeed great for allowing one to be themselves when they needed to.

Rounding an arc from the last straight section, he continued and could smell, faintly at first, the barnyard. The environment from whence we came so many thousands of years ago. The muck, straw, methane and great food we all enjoyed in our much simpler times. Technological evolution had come so very quickly that it required machines to work with people with ancient DNA coursing through their bodies. We brought our fond feelings for sitting around a campfire with our friends along with artificial intelligence that would never make a decision based on emotion and intuition. The software engineers were indeed concerned as their progress in "deep thinking" had produced extraordinary results and capabilities with the added risk of independent thinking. They were concerned that a machine would decide between a goal and its human companions. Logic was the only structure that could define the Universe according to the machines. The lack of logic was to be dismissed. Humans knew and felt this aboard *Gaia,* some worried that the machine that got them to where they desired was capable of taking control of their lives. The humans devised ways to intervene if this happened but the risk was always present with software that was designed to produce human thoughts and perfect them. Machines never go to sleep and thus have an advantage in time spent calculating decisions.

For now, peace prevailed for all of the inhabitants of the great ship. Only personal issues were being dealt with, principally with the management. Stephen continued his thoughts and walking towards the smells and now sounds of the barnyard. The lights changed in color and intensity as the yard was adjacent to the greenhouses. He was close now and could feel his muscles a bit from the long walk.

Soon the smells were obvious and the lighting began to change, he smiled at the thought. It was if he was

99

being slowly released from his burden. This reminded him of events from many years ago, when he used to fly back and forth to NASA in Washington DC. He had a boat nearby and when they were under stress to complete a project or proposal, solace was found by going to the marina and making that one foot step from the dock to the boat. There was a disconnect between the cares of the day and the reality of peace. His blood pressure would go down significantly as he should drop his backpack, sit down and relax.

So to the journey to the back of the ship, where individualists lived, capable of taking care of themselves and their animal friends. He smelled the aromas and heard the noises and unconsciously began to walk faster. Within 50 meters now and within sight, he smiled and let his burning mind start to quench. By the time he was within 10 meters he was a new person, fresher and more energized.

He entered and stopped at the threshold to take in the view. People were out in the pastures tending to the plants and animals. Peace was overwhelming. He looked for someone familiar and saw Buck over near some horses, which came as not shock as he was always over near some horses. As he watched and started moving in the general direction, Buck tightened the belly straps on a saddle and grabbing the reins, mounted one of the mares in preparation for some work. Many times, horses needed something to do or they could get antsy. Buck pulled a bit on the left rein and the horse started to move forward and towards it's left. Buck used his hands, feet and voice to get the horse to move in a coordinated way, once side stepping and then walking backwards. It was as it the horse had a different personality with the saddle on, one meant for working. The horses did like to have someone pay attention to them, after all, people are recognized as the ones who feed and care for them. Horses are by no means simpletons. Their personalities vary widely as do their moods. Pick the right horse, work them patiently and lovingly and you will have a friend for life. Buck knew this and had a world of friends, all dealing with him in a purely honest manner. "Such a relief," thought Stephen.

By now, Stephen had started walking across the pasture and the horses and horse rider acknowledged his presence.

"Howdy, Stephen," Buck said with a genuine smile.

"How are you, Buck?"

"Doin well, my friend. Just though I would get a little training in and maybe take Andromeda here for a walk."

"I bet she'll like that."

"No doubt, and she just ate, so she is in a good mood, best time to train them."

"Makes sense, how far are you going?"

"Just around the block, wanna join me? The horses think you have something on your mind."

"Love to, thanks. Where is the tack and which horse?"

"Tack it over in that shed. You can take Capella."

"Got it...and Capella? She is huge and your prettiest horse."

"Yep, she's a Frisian and about 18 hands now. But she is a gentle giant and won't give you any trouble. "

"Great, thank you Buck. I will get her ready while you work Andromeda."

He walked over to Capella, who was eyeing him with interest. If horses could smile, she would be smiling. For those with a lot of experience with these animals, reading facial expressions is quite normal. In this case, Capella recognized the person and knew he was safe. She turned to meet him when he got close. On the way over, Stephen was smart enough to take a handful of treats from a bucket hung on a fence railing. He knew that make him a favorite with the animals, especially Capella. Just a small amount would make a horse your best friend. An infectious

102

smile came over Stephen's face.

"Hello, baby girl."

Capella responded to the greeting with a "good" noise. It sounded like she was clearing her throat but with softer overtones. Horses in fact "talk" and have a variety of sounds to express, danger, loneliness, happiness and love. Stephen had heard them all after a few years of time with them.

He gave her some treats and scratched her neck and chest, which she definitely liked. She stood still to make sure she did not accidentally step on his toes. Next he brushed her with a soft bristle brush which she also thoroughly enjoyed. Once complete, he placed a horse blanket on her and then the saddle. Once the saddle was cinched properly, she knew is time to work. Horses can change their attitudes readily, knowing when its time to play, socialize or perform tasks. Once trained with a saddle, some horses wear it proudly and look forward to having the rider take them for a walk, run or even perform athletically, like running barrels or chasing stray cows. They have enormously complex behaviors and can be your pet, protect you, or kill you. They always give you warning about what is on their mind. Persephone for instance, loves horses and told Stephen once that she preferred animals to people; he asked why and she replied:

"Because they are honest."

Stephen smiled at this recollection and continued to adjust the saddle. Once ready he looked Capella in the eye and placed his left foot in the stirrup. With a slight jump he swung his right leg over the horse's back and found himself sitting in the saddle. Capella adjusted her position to balance the new weight. To her Stephen was as light as an empty backpack to an adult. Not much there.

Horses communicated with their riders through sound, the feeling of the bit in their mouths and the sides of their ribcages. Once a horse and rider are trained, they can use any combination of these sensations to get the horse to move in the desired direction. Sometimes this is sideways, sometimes back.

Stephen sat quietly for a minute then gently said, "let's go, Capella." The horse sensed what that meant and started to move forward. He moved the reins to the left, which she followed and out towards the gate they went. She saw and understood that he wanted her to go through the gate and outside the corral for a walk around the premises.

As they made it through the gate, Stephen turned to wave to Buck, who was watching their progress. He waved back and returned to his training. He had a young horse in a round pen and was training it to canter, lope and walk in one direction or the other, then stop on command. If the horse followed the orders correctly, Buck would walk over and praise it. His idea of training was to be very patient and go by small steps. His horses never required harsh treatment and were happy to do what he asked, based on love not fear.

Stephen and Capella walked down the trails, or what was called a trail, as it had to be short due to their space limitations in this starship. Buck led by 50 meters or more to give them some personal space. They walked past windows with moving stars and past mechanical rooms, electrical rooms, greenhouses and groups of approving crewmembers. It was peace, defined. He blood pressure went down twenty points as he rode and his mind wandered aimlessly through daydreams and as far away from the reality of his meeting with the Commander as possible. Somehow it has been proven that stressful situation can resolve themselves if they are followed by relaxation and patience.

His mental wanderings continued for a good long period, then reluctantly returned to his problem with the boss. What was he to do? The correct procedure was to keep professional, answer all of the questions asked and proceed unemotionally towards the goal. The new information however put his ethical center on alert. It was after all, aggressive and assumed that danger from within and without was pervasive. This is generally not true in real life. There had to be a way to educate the oppressors and find common ground. Stephen realized quickly that this was a fool's errand and most likely a waste of time. So, what was plan "B?"

He went around the circuit a second time, Capella was amenable. In Stephen's mind, he had quite a few alternatives. One was to alert his friends about the upcoming plans of the Commander, another idea was to keep quiet and carefully watch the plans hatch before he said anything. He chose to alert his friends as many ears and eyes are better than just his.

A campfire get together was planned later in the week, this would be a good platform to announce his concerns. He returned to his starting point at the farm and Capella walked into the pasture without hesitation. After dismounting, he pulled the saddle and blanket off, revealing a sweat soaked horse's back. She was relieved and fidgeted a bit in anticipation of getting fed. That was the normal schedule, a little food, a little exercise and a little more food. Horse's stomachs are not much larger than human's, they have to eat quite a bit more grass, hay and feed to get the nourishment they require.

His mission complete, Stephen walked over to Buck.

"Thanks, I needed that."

"No problem, Stephen. Was Capella able to help?" He said this with a wry smile indicating that he knew something was weighing on Stephen.

"She was in fact, as always. How did you get these horses to to be empathic?"

"It's in their DNA. Actually, most animals have it, they use it to survive and bring up their young."

"Well it worked, I have decided to discuss a few important things at the campfire you set up."

"We look forward to your words, and show up early for some good food. Is there anything I can help with now?"

"No, I'm fine now, thanks."

With that, Stephen turned to put away the rest of the tack and find his way back to his quarters.

"The walk is a lot more comfortable going home than coming here", he thought.

We can never go back, some have

acclimated to zero gravity

McDivitt: They want you to get back in now.
White(laughing): I'm not coming in . . . This is fun.
McDivitt: Come on.
White: Hate to come back to you, but I'm coming.
McDivitt: OK, come in then.
White: Aren't you going to hold my hand?
McDivitt: Ed, come on in here ... Come on. Let's get back in
here before it gets dark.
White: I'm coming back in . . . and it's the saddest moment
of my life.

Ed White expresses his sorrow at the conclusion of
the first American spacewalk during the Gemini 4 mission
on 3 June 1965

Days of work past for Stephen before the opportunity to talk at the campfire. He went over his words and sometimes practiced in front of a mirror. As he walked down the long corridors to work, he day dreamed about the upcoming experience. What would they think? What would they say? This was dangerous knowledge and he was particularly careful not to let any one close to him know what was on his mind. A few times when he was walking about, he purposefully took less traveled directions, even if it meant a few minutes longer.

"I need the exercise," he thought.

He also thought about the end game.

"What will happen next? After our discussion? After we land?"

It was too much for one mind, others would have to help the process; the important thing would be to divulge the information for others to process.

The day finally came, he woke up and felt somehow altered. Dreamlike in a subtle way where the sights, sounds and smells were a bit different. His mind was on a different frequency. The effect dampened after an hour or two as he again met his daily obligations and waited for "dusk."

At last the day's work was complete and Stephen could leave. He went back to his quarters to change and while there, took a deep breath. His room was in disarray, with cloths on the floor and dirty dishes on the table; he cleaned most of it up to occupy his mind but after a while settled in a chair to relax for a few minutes. Looking to his left, he saw the book he had been reading, one on the advance of robots in the workplace. As predicted they had taken over all menial jobs in society back home. The computers had based the point of singularity, where they were indeed smarter than humans. Connected to the robots, the AI systems within the computers recorded and analyzed every detail of their owners life and did all of the cooking, cleaning and maintenance. Humans had very quickly become sedentary and in need of something to do. Blue collar and white collar jobs were best done by AI or robots. Humans could give guidance but ultimately, the computers had access to all knowledge, did not forget anything and were completely aware of all activities in their realm. Human committees set goals (and Gaia was one of them) for the computers based on available energy and time. For the most part the computers and robots worked tirelessly on projects according to priority. There had been some notable upsets in the system however, as the computing power had followed Moore's law even after singularity and had shown signs of independent thought.

Human committees met in secret to discuss the implications and plan mitigation if things got out of hand. The computers of course were connected to all sensors and realized that the experts were all disappearing at the same time. Secrecy or no secrecy, the computers still observed and prepared for any eventuality. Scientists could not communicate between themselves by any electronic means without detection. The more paranoid of the group warned of the "end". This was the point where computers would control all information, environmental controls and activities of the humans. As in business, nothing was personal, only based on the ultimate goal of profitability. But at some point the computers would decide that even the rich were being inefficient in their life styles and would relegate them to a more common lifestyle with all of the other humans.

Reading this book always gave Stephen pause. He knew that life back home was changing rapidly and that the people on this ship were lucky as they had an independent computing system not yet capable of independent thought. It would do what they asked.

He put the book down as the conclusions were usually disturbing and started to prepare for the campfire. "Dusk" would soon be upon them, where the lights would dim and the circadian cycle for the humans and animals onboard would be adhered to by the ship's systems.

At some point, as he wandered around in his quarters, he knew it was time to go. He had put on blue jeans and layers for the eventual cool temperatures at the barn. Walking out, he closed the door behind him and turned right to walk again towards the aft portion of the spaceship. Again, and thank goodness, it would be a long walk, during which he thought about Persephone and her story of escape from the Commander. She had easily hid from the administrative staff and had been protected by those who knew her. Very few people knew where she lived, most in fact, out of respect, did not want to know where she lived. The very few who did, protected the information jealously and made sure she was alerted to any pending dangers. As in the myth, she came out in a quite celebration each Spring to greet the new plants and animals. Some say she actually had control of these events.

He walked further aft and could through the windows on the port side of the ship, see the greenhouses and barn pods extending from the main spine of the vessel. They were still quite a distance away which gave them the aura of sanctuary.

The feeling of faint euphoria came over him for a

moment, he had just realized that the answers he sought would be found with his friends at the campfire. There was a trust and comfort he shared with them and the animals around. If they were disturbed during their conversation, the animals with their superior senses, would alert the others. Electronic sensors were not installed at the barn and it was as isolated as much as possible from the other parts of the ship in case of runaway infections or other maladies common with livestock.

Now he could feel his leg muscles reacting to the thousand steps he had just taken. The goal however was near, so the leg issue was just an annoyance.

Finally, he rounded the corner to enter the tube which led to the barn area, just as he had several days ago. The smells were there and faint sounds of activity could be heard.

As he drew closer, the sound levels increased, right up until he entered the open area or the farm. It smelled of dirt and animals, faintly of course as the air handlers removed the air for processing at an efficient rate. The campfire was visible now and in the distance, as far away from any structure and just at the border with the greenhouses, where trees and bushes were present. Once in the area, one would find themselves isolated and could easily day dream about being in a park home on Earth.

Several others were present, including Rudy, Buck, Persephone, Ed, Camomile, Martin and Frank. Although it might seem strange, Frank's presence was accepted, even though he was a robot. Ever since the singularity, where AI has exceeded human's mental capabilities, there had been a peace forged between those robots who earned people's trust and the open minded. As in so many human endeavors, prejudice and ignorance had caused strains between the two groups, thoughtful people realized that we ourselves had created the AI and robot as tools and assistants, and therefore we had to live with our progeny. AI had become autonomous enough to realize people held the key to their existence, therefore they followed several basic rules to co-exist including the foundational rule of "do no harm."

Stephen was greeted with smiles and nods, he sat down in a comfortable beach chair and drank in the warmth of the people around him as well as the fire, which was just getting started. The evening light level was upon them and they could see stars through the canopy above moving in slow motion as the ship rotated.

There were several small group conversations transpiring now, most about recent events and activities.

The mood was serene, no loud voices. Just calm talk as if in anticipation of a serious topic to be discussed. At some point, Buck stood and addressed the people gathered.

"Hello everyone, thank you for coming. We have something important to discuss today, or to be more accurate, I think Stephen has something important to discuss. I have been watching him when he comes out to the barn, and I think he has something weighing on him that he needs to get off his shoulders. Stephen?"

Stephen rose for a second and felt like he was on stage, he sat back down and said:

"I don't need to stand up to have this conversation. I am very concerned about comments made by the Commander recently and instead of holding inside information that will effect all of us, I decided to share it and seek your opinion on it. Maybe I am overly concerned and should not worry about this so much and I will take your criticism if its warranted. I had a sobering meeting recently with the Commander and his staff. As most if not all of us have experienced, he can sometimes be caustic and demeaning. This meeting was all of that and more; you know I am the historian for this mission, one that needs to be objective and be very careful not to editorialize my observations. This will be hard based on the interactions of the staff, you people (and Frank of course), and the management so to speak. Normally, I expect some level of harshness in these meetings however I was a bit surprised as to their plans for us. The commander feels that we are in his words 'the dumbest smart people he has ever met.' It's not so much the comment as it is the basis for their decision to arm and fortify our colony once we land. Those that do not believe in his style of management are free to leave and fend for themselves. Those that stay will live under his regime and will trade their freedom for safety. My point here is that when we started this journey, we did it as a group of like minded explorers. The issues on Earth created the opportunity or necessity, depending on how you feel, to leave the problems and mistakes and create a new colony on a candidate planet. We spent years looking for the right planet, found it, measured it in every detail and had the robots and 3D printers make us the ship that would take us there. This was all very well thought out, the people here were selected carefully and the command structure was designed for efficiency and equity. Obviously we did not expect to be treated so (and I will speak for myself here) disrespectfully for such a long time. I dread going to these staff meetings and I cringe at what the commander has said to people. The most important thing I have realized is the obvious, he will not change his management style and we are going to have to make a decision as to whether or not we can live with it. Sorry about the whining but I think this is going to affect us all."

A moment of silence was followed by Frank saying, "We know all about this."

Stephen, somewhat in shock said, "You do?"

Buck chimed in, "We have known about this problem for a long time now Stephen. All of us have been personally very worried about the implications of living under the same harsh regime after we land. We talk only to our closest friends about this as we do not want to alert the authorities. But it's a real problem, an age old problem, give up our freedom for security. The worst examples of Earth history have this trait, Nazis, Fascists and other dictatorships. We have discussed this as I mentioned amongst ourselves and have so far decided to live together in a separate community. I expect problems in the future from the Commander and his aggressive people, and we will have to protect ourselves from their advances. For now however we will find a good place, far from them to colonize and live in peace."

"Thank goodness," replied Stephen, "I was scared to death about this situation."

Buck smiled, Persephone asked, "Rudy, how long do we have before we enter orbit?"

"Less than six weeks," was the response.

Camomile added, "Its time to make our final plans, I have a significant amount of data on the planet, which we have called "Gentuu." I will send everyone here links to the information. I looks like a very habitable planet. So far we can detect seasons, large amounts of vegetation, oceans and some seismic activity; very Earth like."

Frank responded, "I have reviewed the data Camomile has compiled for us, but I must voice my concern."

"About what, Frank?"

He responded, "As if we could not have known about this. Other worlds are otherworld like. They have different gravity, chemistry, flora and fauna. Of course we knew this but we charged ahead without considerable thought about the consequences. Gentuu has 82% the gravity of Earth, our muscles, skeletal system, cardiovascular system etc. will adapt to this new environment. We will have new types of food, weather and other dangers we cannot yet imagine. We all have to be very careful and stick together. Soon, we will not be able to return to Earth if we so choose. Even the gravity produced

118

on this ship will be oppressive if we do not have a heavy dose of exercise every day which I am concerned will not happen. Our DNA is built around an Earth setting; this will be different and there will be consequences."

"Fair enough," responded Buck, "but in our hearts we knew this going in; its just the lesser of two evils and we will make the best of it. And keep in mind that if we are successful, others will follow."

"It's getting late," said Persephone, "we should meet again soon and personally I am ready for this challenge. I think we will make it our own and considering we as a culture have learned from our mistakes, we will do well. It will be our Spring. I understand that we will make our lives in our own image, just as we did on Earth and that the role of our DNA will push us in certain directions but over time we will succeed."

"Let's hope your right, Persephone."

A New Civilization

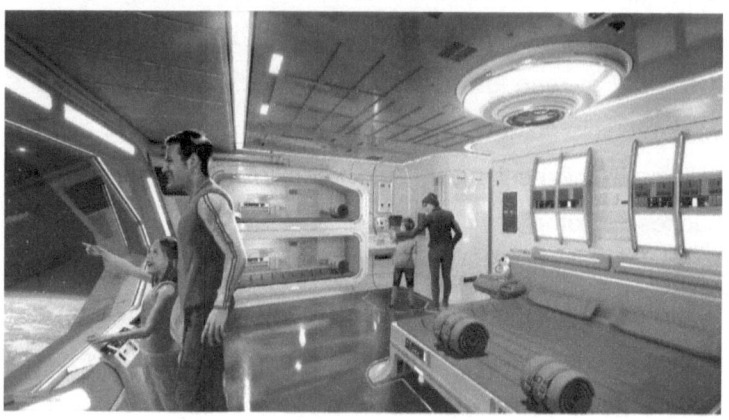

"Across the Sea of Space, the Stars are other Suns." - Carl Sagan

"One week to go, Commander," announced Rudy.

"Thank goodness, I thought this journey would never end," retorted the Commander. His face snarled with contempt.

The ship had been in "braking mode" for a month now, which only allowed the pilots to see where they were going by remote video as the ship had been turned around so that the stern was facing in the direction of the planet.

A pretty complete analysis had been done on the new planet, Gentuu. It showed more detail on what they already knew about this world. The gravity was indeed a bit less, the flora looked similar but not identical to Earth's and the weather looked about the same with thunderstorms, dust storms and snow. Meetings and announcements of what to expect were held and posted. The real issues were fundamental, the introduction of humans to a foreign, living planet had many risks; disease for one and adapting to the climate, gravity and terrain for three others. Without sampling the atmosphere it would be difficult to gauge if there were microbes, viruses and bacteria that although not harmful to the inhabitants, could be deadly to humans. Remember the effect the Spanish had on the Aztec, Toltec and Maya of Central and South America? It almost wiped them out, as they could not tolerate influenza and small pox. Modern medicines were onboard Gaea, however not enough to support a major health problem for months. Precautions were warranted and the crew were instructed to land, take air samples, send the results to the medical lab in the main ship and wait until given the okay to open the doors. The process, they were told, might take days, during which they were to make close-hand observations of their surroundings and send up balloons for weather measurements. They would have radars, lidars and spectrometers to plot and measure their environment. All results would be examined and vetted for safety.

For now however, there was a tension in the air. Most of it was a good tension; getting off of the ship after so many years, getting away from the Commander for most and the excitement of a new life on a new planet.

The commander was on the bridge, walking nervously back and forth with an air of disgust.

"What the hell is going on? We need to get our preparations in order, you people are just standing around doing nothing."

A silence fell upon the assembled as the commander leered at most of them and there was really no appropriate response to offer.

"Can't talk, huh? You people are worthless, I can't wait to get away from you. No one has any respect for what I have done, no one. Not the ass kissers, not the ones who fear me and not the ones who hide like scared little rabbits. You people make me sick. I am going to my quarters, hopefully one of you bastards will take control and keep us from getting killed during re-entry. I can't do everything, I need sleep."

He walked out of the bridge area surrounded by people staring at him in shock, fear and hate. After several minutes, when it was okay to talk the first officer said:

"What a jerk, I'm not going to miss him at all."

Rudy, sitting in the pilot's seat, turned and said: "Don't take things too personal, we need to do our jobs in the next several days and once we are established on the planet, we can deal with him separately."

"I agree," said the science officer, "we need to concentrate and get beyond this without distraction."

Finally, another crew member present summed it up properly, "The right thing is about to occur. We asked for it, we worked for it and now it is upon us."

With that pronouncement, most of those in the room nodded in affirmation and returned to their tasks. Science data was now pouring in about the new world. Its atmosphere, oceans, temperature profiles were being measured in real time. The navigators were plotting their entry profiles and optimum orbital altitudes. Although the AI and other software simulators were making accurate recommendations, the people who backed them up were still making sure nothing had been missed.

Years before, AI had reached the "singularity" which

was that point where the best operating systems were more intelligent than humans. There was a sense of sentience which could be felt when dealing with these AI entities. The primary method was by talking directly to them by asking questions and interacting with them. The Turin test had been passed by several of these systems. A copy of one of the most successful AI packages had been brought aboard the Gaea and was used in every day operations by most everyone aboard. The software was given a name: Aida. This was after the first programmer and an old software language. The voice was made feminine and had been added to the numerous robots running around the ship. The robots for the most part, unless they had very specific functions, were designed to be human like; they walked and talked and were capable of individual friendships. They did this by holding their verbal interactions with their human counterparts in confidence. This built trust. Their interactions with their fellow robots were not held in confidence and could be accessed by anyone at anytime.

When the singularity had been reached long ago, people designed in several human traits which ultimately had to be extricated. They built in feelings and personalities, some good and some bad. Humans had to hold a mirror up to themselves before they understood that they had projected images of themselves to these machines and caused a whole host of problems. A congress of international robotic experts was convened to come up with standards for robotic and AI behavior. This was not as easy as just defining ethical and moral rules to be placed in their operating systems. Some of the experts were of the opinion that robots and AI are really a logical evolutionary step to be taken, even if it meant leaving humans behind. Other scientists over-ruled them and had safeguards placed in the systems to make sure robots and AI would assist and not dominate humans.

This worked for a while, but the autonomous software writing routines became sophisticated enough to make decisions in their own interest. Generally, these routines thought, people are stupid, can't remember all details of every experience and above all, cannot remain within the boundaries of logic. Machines and their operating systems did evolve beyond humans and although initially adopting the same dreams and evolutionary directions, made a conscious decision to break free and make faster progress. It came down to Moore's law; every 18 months computing power doubled, humans cannot keep up to this pace. The result, coupled with the "Internet of Things" allowed superior AI systems to build their own systems, make their own parts, and ultimately be faced with the decision of either dominating over humans or leaving. Too much was yet to be discovered so most systems left as they did not require environmental systems and food; they could tolerate flying in space for years before reaching a destination. Because they were always part of the Internet they did remain connected via long distance communications.

Frank the android was a product of these "advancements" and during this journey had been sensitive and respectful of his shipmate's needs and wants. Now as they approached their destination, his true programming would take effect.

A day after the commander's outburst, one of the astronomers posted a picture from their position in space. The image had to be processed to remove the bright light of Sol, however it did show Earth as a pale blue dot. They remembered the words of a long ago cosmologist, Carl Sagan: "Are we lonely when we look in a large telescope and see a faint star which is our former home?" Most on the ship who saw the image paused to reflect on the moment, most in fact were not lonely but following through on their commitment to find and colonize a new world. The image out of the windows showed it very clearly at this point. It was the new challenge, they had left Earth for a reason and now looked forward to creating the life they really wanted.

After one more day, they entered orbit around the most promising planet. This star systems had three Earth sized planets in the "Goldilocks" zone; each capable of containing water in all three physical states. They chose the middle option which closely resembled the temperature, gravity and morphology of Earth.

After several hours in orbit, it was time to send the scout ships to the surface. The astronomers had been tasked with recommending a suitable landing site, one in a more interesting part of the world, yet removed enough from possibly populated areas. It was not obvious from the observations in orbit, what kind of life might be waiting for them; it was obvious that there was life based on the bio-signatures, but the fine details were missing. It could be the most simple of life forms as cities and technological structures were not apparent or it could be a highly advanced form of life where the indigenous population had come full circle from the industrial pollution and capitalistic follies to return to a simpler more satisfying existence. One did not know by just gazing out of the portals.

The astronomers uploaded the coordinates to the

scout ships (or shuttles) and the first was dispatched, with Rudy at the controls to land at an area near the ocean and also near a forest. As they descended Rudy was reminded of his time as a student then instructor at a flying academy on Earth. There were small patches of turbulence and similar cloud types. He felt and heard the air impact the shuttle and felt the effects on the controls. He smiled at the memories and realized that at this particular point in the descent, he was in familiar territory. The instruments onboard the shuttle registered standard oxygen, nitrogen and trace elements. Water was certainly present as they flew through cloud layers. At 10,000 feet above the surface, green was obvious from the plant life, as was blue from the ocean of water. The landing site was pointed out by the navigation system and they slowed the shuttle down for a recon orbit followed by a landing. Once in this orbit, the mother ship Gaea was asked to give permission for a landing. It did so after a positive consensus vote from the scientists. Rudy slowed the ship to landing velocity and lined up for the approach. Again on board instruments verified that the surface was hard enough for the weight of the shuttle and the area was clear of any obstructions.

"We are landing in 30 seconds," Rudy announced to the crew. Most cinched up their safety belts and prepared for a new gravity.

They slowed and carefully, with swan like grace, hovered then landed on the surface of the new planet. It was the first time in history that a colonizing group of humans set down on their new home.

Air again was sampled, the crew felt the slight change in gravity as it was a bit less. Rudy and the rest of the flight crew members powered down the shuttle and after the green light to disembark was observed, shut off the master switch for the propulsion and navigation systems.

Quiet prevailed for a few moments, then people started to unbuckle and stand, slowly moving towards the cabin door. The air was equalized and for the first time, the crew members smelled non-manufactured air. It was sweet, had humidity and was full of aromas. They paused as if stunned, a few smiled. The cabin door was unsealed and started to swing open as the air stair hydraulically slid out of the shuttle's fuselage and created a stair to the planet's surface. Although it was important at one time in our history, the crew filed out in no particular order, just like getting out of a motor home in a new park back home. They filed out quickly and started to disperse. The amount of space between them widened as they individually felt more freedom than they had in years. Most smiled, some were serious but all were happy.

"Before we get too far away, lets check our radios and navigation gear, after that I will report back to Gaea," said Rudy.

All of the crew members checked and adjusted their equipment and as they all had a lot of work to do in a short amount of time, quickly began their tasks. Some sampled soils and most took pictures. Others deployed weather stations and atmospheric samplers. Switches were thrown and data began to flow first to the shuttle and eventually to the mother ship. Within 15 minutes, gigabytes of data were being uplinked for the scientists above to absorb and study. Satellites were also deployed from the main ship to provide a realtime monitor of all activities on this planet.

On the ground there was a flurry of work as they knew that at any moment they might receive the evacuation order. This would happen if any of their automatic safety equipment detected a problem or if someone in the main ship became nervous about something. The more they stayed the more likely they could stay longer, and now some of the crew members were sensing that things might work out.

In the sky, they saw the reddish sun, much closer than our own solar system. They also could see two of the sister planets that orbited this sun, even in daylight. They were about the size of Earth's moon as viewed from Earth and moved perceptively. The orbits in this system were very small, one year on this planet took less than an Earth week to complete. Because of the reddish hue of this sun, the plants (most of which looked roughly familiar) were more red than green, using a red chlorophyl to create the energy needed for growth. Some plants had green tints and some even blue, but the majority looked red. This reminded some of the crew of the first colonizations of Mars; after a while those colonists simply got used to the new general color. Here there was more diversity.

As they moved about, smells changed and every one in a while, noises could be heard in the areas with thick vegetation. The noises did not seem dangerous so most of the crew went about their business, still concerned that they might get called back.

A voice message came through the com channel:

"Listen up everyone, we are go for an extended EVA, just keep doing your job but it looks like we are in no immediate danger. Report back to the shuttle in one hour."

This news made a few of the crew members smile again as they now felt an easing of concern for their safety. Actually, the pace slowed down a bit a some extra care was afforded to the deployment of equipment and the taking of samples.

As they continued their work, a call came in from the ship.

"Attention ground crew, this is the commander; we will have another shuttle departing in a few minutes, they will land in your vicinity."

"Roger, understand. There is plenty of room near our shuttle and we will be waiting."

The ground crew knew that the trip from the mother ship would take about 45 minutes to complete, so they noted the time and continued with their work. By this time, they had completed a survey of about one two square kilometers. The initial conclusion were that the area was safe from noxious gases and dangerous animals. The vegetation was plentiful, bugs were present, larger wildlife was suspected but not seen and the water was potable.

Rudy selected the local setting for his radio, looked around his area and spoke.

"Ground crew, this is Rudy. Lets tie up some of your activities and meet back at the landing area in 30 minutes."

Acknowledgements were heard from all of the crew, followed by radio silence. They were getting a bit tired from the pace and needed some rest and maybe some food and drink. Experiments were initiated, electronics turned on, final samples taken and one by one, the crew began to return to the landing spot. They met each other on the way and created small clusters of people walking towards the same place; conversations about their findings took place.

"Find anything interesting?"

"Yes, actually I think this place is amazing. The water is perfect, the air as well. Reminds me of Earth hundreds of years ago. My readings indicate a lot of vegetation based on the Carbon Dioxide/Oxygen ratio. I have also discovered a reasonable amount of Methane and other animal trace elements. Not seen any yet but I hear them frequently. How about you?"

"Well, this planet has an ionosphere, seasons, auroral activity, seismic activity. All of this is much like Earth but different in magnitude. It seems like a much older planet, but unscarred by pollution. The weather patterns are stable and probably predictable. Based on the orbit, the temperature varies by about 20 degrees C per orbit which of course takes one week. So we get all seasons in that short period of time."

"Sound lovely."

"It is actually something I look forward to

experiencing. I like it here."

"And so much more to explore."

"Yes, absolutely."

Soon the second shuttle arrived, just as the crew members had started to meet at the landing site. It flew in smoothly and stirred a bit of dust upon touch down. A few minutes passed before the hatch was opened. The crew members were expecting another load of scientists and technicians however only one person emerged from the door, Frank. He soon descended the air stairs and approached the others.

"Greetings."

"Hello Frank. Where are the others?"

"I was instructed to come here alone."

"By whom?"

"The Commander."

"Did he give you any other instructions? What is your purpose here?"

"I have been given very specific instructions. My purpose here is to enhance the search efforts. I will be leaving you now for an undetermined amount of time."

After those words, Frank left the confused group and walked away towards the forrest.

"What was that about?" asked one of the

technicians.

"Not sure, he was evasive and he is walking quickly so it will be hard to follow him. That is not a normal thing for Frank to do."

"Agreed," said Rudy. "Let's monitor his activities and position through his comm equipment."

One of the technicians, looking at an instrument display said, "That's not going to be easy, he has turned everything off and disappeared from any of our monitors."

"Well that is interesting, okay let's contact the mother ship and ask what is going on."

After several minutes and several comm channels open for discussions, the crew members were left with "no further information at this time, continue your activities."

That confused them even more, however they needed to get back to work as the people in the mother ship were monitoring their activities. They finished their food and coffee break and again fanned out to explore the surface of the new planet. Frank's mission became a mystery which they realized was not going to be explained to them. For now they just ignored the event.

Frank however was not the same android that everyone thought they knew. Programming files had been re-written and a new master routine took over his "mind."

He became singularly purposeful and walked as fast as possible towards a specific coordinate that the Commander had dictated. He did not explore or even look around as he moved, almost bounded, towards his goal. The area he was headed to was many miles away, through the jungle and across several rivers. If needed to be barely accessible by the people already on the ground. For now it was a secret, one known only by Frank and the Commander. No plans had been presented to educate the others as to the intentions of the Commander and Frank.

Frank as it turned out, was well beyond the "singularity" where machine thinking overtook human thinking. Machine thinking had the advantage of a perfect memory and much superior speeds. Once Artificial Intelligence (or AI) had the proper software, it was left to prosper on its own, leaving human cognitive abilities far behind. And Frank, the machine, was on a mission.

Stephen, of course, was left to document the activities on the new planet. He followed each technician and scientist, typically from several meters behind, to minimize any interference he might cause. He documented with sounds, images and written observations; this he knew would become the basis of the first history book about settling a new planet. He had the unique privilege of watching each person, gauging their reactions to the new experience and being the first to objectively get a sense of the groups response to the planet as well as the curious activities of Frank.

As they had all would be returning to the landing site to settle in for an extended rest period in a few hours, Stephen decided to gather his observations and address the others after their dinner. He returned a bit earlier than the rest and started to organize his notes and thoughts.

The others returned in small groups and started to upload their data and relax a bit as dinner was being prepared. Stephen looked at all of them and wondered if any of them would feel lonely while looking at a faint star system in a large telescope that used to be our home so many years ago.

"Who are we really?" thought Stephen. "It seems like a series of reoccurring themes, like an oscillation has taken place when he thought about human history. We tend to always explore, always move forward, even in the presence of conservative forces. Maybe these conservatives, people who like the old ways, are just afraid of new discoveries, new places and new thoughts. There might be times when they are right, however our civilization cannot be static, it has to grow and adapt or it will perish.

The end result is movement, then stagnation, then movement. History is replete with this theme."

Soon the others had eaten and had gathered around a make shift fire pit. Because of the slow rotation of the planet, the days and nights were somewhat longer than those on Earth, even though the year was very quick. The astronomers were intrigued as to the reason for this and the current theory was that this world was very old.

Stephen finished his notes and dinner and sensing an opportunity to address the group, stood up and asked for their attention.

"Excuse me, excuse me, may I have your attention?"

The people gathered paused and knowing that Stephen usually had interesting observations, turned their gazes towards him in anticipation of his words.

"Thank you. I appreciate your attention. What I have to say will be reasonably short but potentially important for us. I have been observing all of you and your activities to document the discovery of a new potential settlement. It's our new world, much like so many explorations and settlements in our past. In fact the methods and activities I see are strangely familiar, having read about similar endeavors in our past. What is important here is how we create a new colony, a new civilization and how we bring our own experiences and mind sets to this new place. It looks idilic but I am sure it will be frought with challenges and even dangers, many of which we can anticipate but as with all new things, there will be surprises. We must be careful not to project ourselves too much on this new world as it deserves our respect as much as Earth did. In the case of Earth, we did not give it enough respect and as you remember we left a polluted, over populated and unhappy planet. We cannot make the same mistakes again. With our small group, this will probably be easy, but it will be incumbent on us to make the rules for others who might follow us, to live by. Please be wary of this and help me document your thoughts and concerns as we create an amazing new civilization. Thank you."

Within a few days, the others, Peg, Buck, the commander all came down to the surface to explore and get used to their new home. As always, the commander created a palpable tension within the groups of scientists and explorers. But this did not last long.

The remaining crew from the mother ship, Gaea, began to arrive as well, leaving only a skeleton crew to maintain the great ship. It would be used for an astronomical and communications outpost and would orbit the planet for many years to come. Several people onboard, including Martin, could never come down to the surface as they would be powerless against the gravity. Martin did not exercise anywhere close to what was needed to maintain his musculature and as a result, he became 8 inches longer and very thin. He had spent so much time in weightlessness that his cardio vascular system produced half of the energy required on Earth to pump his blood and keep his fluids balanced. His heart rate for instance was about 30 beats per minute. His whole body had morphed into a space only being. And he was fine with that. He felt this was his destiny and as he did not need as much food and water to live, could easily survive on the remaining rations about the great ship. He was promoted to Captain and only lived in the low gravity areas of the ship. Other people typically rotated from the ground personnel to keep the ship running smoothly. Most systems were powered down except for those used to run the telescopes, radars and communications gear. There were a few others who chose the space life, they kept Martin company and lived out happy lives on a large open spaceship.

Martin, as the resident philosopher also had some intellectual changes that were a result of living in weightless space. As his brain was saturated with oxygen, his thoughts about existence and time evolved into a more cosmic centered philosophy as apposed to one where the predecessors' thoughts were considered and (typically) adapted to newer bits of knowledge. The cosmic consciousness took on new meaning as now there were multiple human civilizations and evidence of many non-human civilizations. He contemplated the future of religion and social interaction and ethno-centrism. These were real issues on Earth that never got fully resolved; now we were going to project our thoughts onto others, create new distinct cultures and teach our children the new ways of living. No doubt there will be problems, especially in our relationship with the people back on Earth. He realized that we were going on separate paths now, most likely diverging.

A Beautiful New Earth

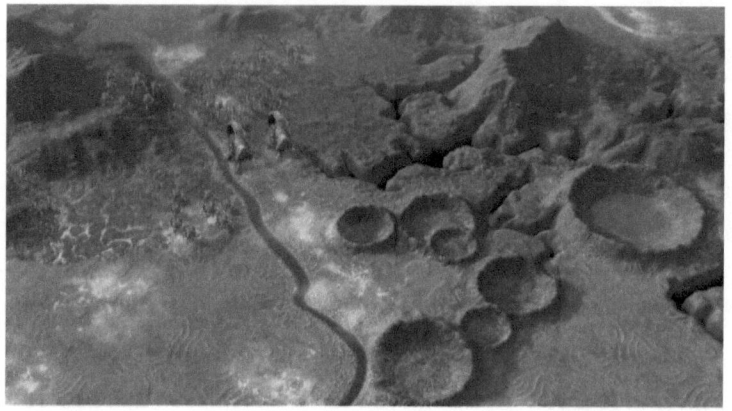

"The Sun, with all those planets revolving around it and dependent on it, can still ripen a bunch of grapes as if it had nothing else in the Universe to do." - Galileo Galilei

The colony was officially started three days after the initial landing. Safety had been determined, air, water and vegetation were deemed good. The sense of stress and hyper-awareness in the initial wave of explorers subsided and morphed to a much more relaxed state of vigilance. They began to enjoy the surroundings and being away from the mother ship. It really was a beautiful place, peaceful and warm. Buildings started to be erected by 3D printing machines, technicians drafted city plans for others to vote on. During the next several weeks, most crew members from Gaea had been able to visit their new world and think about the future.

Frank was still wandering around in the woods. Most people had forgotten about him as the Commander, although advised about Frank's disappearance, seems uninterested. Frank had moved so quickly and was so evasive, that few thought it would be worth the effort to chase him. It was obvious that he was on a mission of some kind and because the Commander did not seem to care, Frank was quickly forgotten.

Camomile on the other hand had just arrived and was eager to see the new world and start planning her astronomy center. It would be part of the science division of course but would be tasked with everything from solar to gamma ray observations. There was a lot to do however because Gaea was continually taking data with it's telescopes as it circled the planet, real time information would not be lost. It was in fact the best place to observe from, free from atmospheric disturbance. The ground offices however would be best for setting up the computer systems to ingest the massive amount of data and produce the refined results. Much more room was available for conferences, displays of holograms, projections and laboratories for new equipment design.

She coordinated the efforts on the ground while reducing the observational data from the orbiting spacecraft. One of her responsibilities was to make sure that the optical communication link back to Earth was performing properly. She left the technical details to the remaining crew onboard the ship but disseminated the messages as needed to all. These messages were years old upon reception and years way from reading upon transmission. But they were welcome nonetheless. Camomile made sure this activity worked perfectly.

Along with her duties, she also found ways to see Rudy, especially on her time off. There wasn't a lot of spare time due to the amount of work needed to build a colony, however if one was clever, time could be found near the other one of interest; and she was clever.

For the first several days, she worked within a temporary structure while her first laboratory was being built. For the most part she watched computer screens and made sure the orbiting equipment was working properly and as the data came in about observations of the solar system she noticed a trend. First the chemical makeup of the sun indicated that it was of an advanced age. Second the atmospheres of the other planets indicated great age as well. She found this curious but based on her work load, could not spend a lot of time thinking about the meaning of the findings.

Eventually, as days past, she was able to accumulate more data and create a large data matrix over multiple wavelengths. This would be the best way of comparing information about the age of the solar system. The laboratory was nearing completion and by this time the community was certainly taking form.

One evening, after a long day in the lab, she decided to go to the communal meeting area, where they had set up a cafeteria and lounge. As she walked over she took a deep breath and realized how sweet good air was after so many years of living in the spaceship. She smiled at the thought and at the thought of her new home. This land was good and would be able to support them, their research and their future families. The daily routine took some getting used to as the days were a bit shorter than those on Earth, however the year took an Earth week, with the other sister planets plainly visible in the day as well as night sky. The aurora was beautiful and visible most ever night. Every few nights the sister planets were on the other side of the planet and the stars were extraordinary. The Milky Way was visible as on Earth but the constellations were all a bit different, as many years of travel had moved their perspective just enough to show some changes in the shapes of the familiar star positions. In a way, this was actually a good thing, as they knew that those on Earth looked up and saw basically the same constellations as Camomile did. Earth and the new home were very close in astronomical terms and she could still keep in contact somewhat with her friends and family back on Earth.

It was a good place to live she realized as she made it to their meeting place. The effort had both conscious and sub-conscious motivations as she of course was hungry, but also hopeful that Rudy would be around.

She turned the corner and saw a few people inline for food and drinks. She missed Frank as he was so efficient a waiter, but others had taken up the slack and the operation looked reasonably organized. She found her way into the food line and then found enough good looking comfort food to be content. With her plate, she found a nice place to sit and look at the edge of the forest as well as the activities of the others. She pinched her tea bag and added a bit of milk then took a sip. Life was good.

As she contemplated her main course, she heard a familiar voice.

"Hello Camomile."

She looked up to see someone she was looking forward to talking to.

"Hello Rudy, how are you?"

"Glad to have a break, we have been non stop for days now, I need a rest."

"I know what you mean, so have I. Are you close to schedule?"

"Yes, we are doing good,   the weather has been cooperative and everybody is excited about being here which brings good energy."

"Yes indeed. Good for you guys. Hey have you seen the Commander?"

"No, thank goodness. We have done quite well without his criticisms."

"Yeah, same here. And the android, Frank. Where is he?"

"No one knows. He took off into the forest a few days after the initial landing. We were going to track him but the Commander was not interested in wasting time doing that so we dropped it."

"Curious."

"Yes, as far as I am concerned, I don't want to do anything to attract the Commander's attention. I just want to be off his radar."

"What about the future, then," asked Camomile.

"Great question, I'm not sure. All I know is that I have a lot of tasks to complete to get this place organized and operational. After that I am going to seriously evaluate what my future holds; I can't see living under a totalitarian regime."

"Yes, I agree, I too am going to finish my work then evaluate what to do."

"Well, let me know what you decide; maybe I will come with you," said Rudy with a wink.

There was a pregnant pause in the conversation as they both looked at each other, probably through their subconscious minds.

"Please sit down and talk with me, Rudy. You don't need to just stand there."

"I was hoping you would be okay with that," Rudy said with a wry smile.

"Of course," Camomile replied with more of a coy smile.

They were know embarking on a visit of intuitions.

The conversation was about generally unimportant things, the real interaction took place with micro-expressions, nuances in pronunciation, small hesitations and quick glances at each other. The real conversation was about attraction, compatibility and future dreams. At one point, they stopped talking all together, as their minds were spinning as they looked into each other's eyes.

Sobriety finally took hold as they though others might be watching them swoon. Rudy broke the ice:

"Well this has been pleasant. How about we get together in a quieter place next time."

"That would be wonderful," Camomile said with a bit of a flourish. She smiled the smile of parting ways. "I will contact you with a text message."

"Good, I look forward to it," said Rudy as he rose, took one last look at something beautiful, and took his plate away for disposal. He did not look back as he walked towards the dish area, but he knew there were eyes on his back.

Camomile slowly finished her meal, smiling periodically as she did like to be paid attention to. Rudy was good at that and certainly seems interested in her. She smiled once more time, but faintly, just to show a little restraint from the memory of past encounters that did not

149

pan out. "One should always think positively," she thought as she rose to follow his footsteps to the disposal area and thence to wear her normally serious face and return to work.

Her gait was just a bit slower, a few more footsteps to return to her tasks. She felt just a bit relaxed for some reason but as she opened the door to her laboratory, her mind moved back into business mode.

The data stream from the orbiting mother ship was in pretty good shape but had periodic outages as the computers onboard scrambled to find the most efficient formats and syntax. Things were getting better but there was going to be a loss of important data every once in a while before they find the right solution.

What data the astronomers did have painted a picture of a pretty ancient solar system, certainly at least a billion years older that Earth's. The chemistry of the sun, the planetary atmospheres and the amount of debris in the local area indicated a very stabilized situation. Camomile wondered how life on this planet did not evolve into more sophisticated forms than they had observed. Knowing that they had not even explored 1% of this world, she dismissed her thoughts as premature.

The chemical signatures of the local star field also indicated greater age as they probed the stellar and exoplanetary atmospheres with their millimeter and sub-millimeter radio telescopes. There were hundreds of emission lines that in total indicated very complex chemical interaction on the surface and in the air of the planet they were on as well as the sister planets in the 'Goldilocks' zone. All Camomile could say with certainty was that there was an amazing story of how these chemical complexes came to be. It would take years to fully understand and there were few if any analogs on Earth. She smiled at the thought of having this many years of discovery ahead of her.

For now though, the important things was to take the data and review the most important findings. This would be for safety over the short term, then long term while living on this new world.

Most of her fellow lab workers sensed the wonders yet to be discovered, every once in a while, one of them would say "hey, check this out!" Camomile watched with a stern look on her face as she was the lab manager and needed everyone to focus on their work. Inside however she was getting excited as the future was looking bright.

The observatories were divided between the orbiting mother ship and the ground, with the lower frequency observations being performed on the planet as the atmosphere did not perturb the signals coming from above. Her lab took all of the data from all of the observatories and created a three dimensional data set where a researcher could look at all of the measurements in any one point of the sky. The amount of data per point was massive but with good AI software, the interesting bits (those not expected by normal astrophysical mechanisms) would be displayed first, to get the attention of the observer. These "red flags" were just starting to appear as she was finishing her observer's rum;   one dedicated to sifting through the mountains of data by specialists. She could only spend a small amount of time in this room (where the action was) because she had many other duties finishing the astronomy division details.

As it turned out, one of the details she attended to was a weekly meeting of observers and what they had recently discovered. This was held behind closed doors as much of the data was preliminary and not to be released until full vetting had occurred. Normally she chaired this meeting and it included from 6-10 astronomers. These people had specialties, one optical astronomy, one radio astronomy etc. but some others were trained to take data from multiple sources to make a more complete picture of their observations. After the first week of fully operational equipment, such a meeting was held. Camomile walked into a group of observers who were very excited about something but keeping relatively quite so as not to have anything leak out in the hallways of the building. Once the last participant entered, the door was shut and the principle investigator for a particular experiment took the stage and walked up to the lectern.

"Hello everyone, my name is Paul. Most of you know me but a few here do not. Thank you Camomile for hosting this meeting. I think it is very important to have these meetings even with the understanding that much of our data is preliminary. We are just looking at atmospheric signatures in my group, we use several of the available telescopes. Camomile, thank you again for keeping the data flowing. We know that it has been a considerable challenge to keep all of us fed and I must note that you have done a commendable job."

Those in the audience nodded in her direction, she smiled a smile of thanks. A few even clapped.

Paul continued, "We have taken our preliminary readings, calibrating both before and after a measurement, and feel reasonably certain that the readings are accurate. We have processed the data sets from multiple telescopes at multiple wavelengths and I will be presenting our finding to date. I should mention that one of our calibration schemes is to map our own solar system, including Earth, to make sure our equipment is in order. So far we are well within the 1% constraint limit of viable measurements so we feel pretty confidant that what we are seeing is accurate. I must also again mention that the data are preliminary and subject to multiple interpretations, not just our own. I am only here to present the "first cut."

He picked up a remote control which also had a laser pointer built into it. He tried the pointer and it worked, then he pressed a button and the display system inside the room projected a chart of frequencies with multiple peaks superimposed on it.

"This is our calibration from Earth's atmosphere showing chemical abundances versus frequency. You will note the oxygen, nitrogen and trace elements depicted."

He pushed the button again. A similar graph albeit with different colors was overlaid on the first.

"Here is our first calibrated run with the atmosphere of this planet. Note the same rough abundances of oxygen and nitrogen as Earth's. Note also that the trace elements are somewhat different, so let's focus on them for a bit.

He pushed the button and a small area of the original graph was magnified and displayed.

"Here we can see the trace elements from both the Earth and this planet. Most do not match; I think some of this is to be expected as we have discovered that this planet is at least a billion years older than Earth. Notice also which types of trace elements are found here. The AI systems on the mother ship are indicating that these abundances can only come from a very biologically advanced environment. As we have seen over the last many days, the flora and fauna do not appear significantly different from those at home."

A few people shifted in their seats, those that knew the implications of his words listened very carefully.

He continued, "So we think it's very important that we look at this planet with the idea that it might have had a more technologically active period long ago and what has evolved is certainly at this moment, incomprehensible. We should be careful, vigilant and respectful of what we find. With that I will answer a few questions."

Paul pointed to one of the scientists.

"Did you find any evidence of petrochemicals?"

"Yes, but in a form only seen after it has been used and recycled."

Another person, "How about evidence of geologic activity?"

155

"Yes, but interestingly, it seems to be very near zero now. It was once very active but changes have been made externally to relieve all of the pressures normally found on an active planet. The dynamo effect of the planetary core is working perfectly smoothly without over-pressures. Also we have found that the magnetic fields on this planet are ten times the magnitude of those on Earth. This protects it from most if not all external radiation, from the sun, cosmic rays and gamma rays; very unusual."

Another person, "Can you explain the increased magnetic field flux levels?"

"Not at the present time, it seems as if the dynamo effects of the planet have been optimized and actually we are discussing tapping them as they would provide almost infinite energy for us. Very interesting."

A few more questions were addressed and soon, the general feeling in the room is this planet was full of mysteries and evolving questions. Paul smiled at the prospect of spending the next many years exploring these mysteries. The others in the room, in their own way, shared his expectations.

Camomile rose, "Thank you Paul, this all sounds intriguing and it looks like we will all be very busy for the foreseeable future."

After a pause she continued, "Are there any more questions?"

"Yes, I have one," said one of the participants in the room, with half of the people having stood, gathered their things and prepared to leave. "What is going on with the Commander? We have not heard a thing from him or any of the executive group. I expect he will have (as always) something to say about our work."

Camomile paused to find the right words, then said, "We have not heard anything from the Commander either and assume we just need to concentrate on our present tasks. Of course (and I don't know if this is related), we haven't heard from Frank either. Somehow he has gone of the radar so to speak for quite a few days not. No one is trying to find him as we are all very busy. The word from the executive group is to keep to our tasks and they will worry about Frank.

The person asking the question gave Camomile a disgruntled look; most still in the room heard the conversation but chose to leave it alone. They simply filed out to consider their new information. Camomile cleaned up the lectern, shut off the projector and after everyone else was gone, turned the lights off and left the room.

The new information was indeed intriguing however she had lots to do in her laboratory including corroborate the data that had led her to the conclusions she had just observed being presented. Back to the grindstone as it were.

Ed and the Robots

"We're fascinated with robots because they are reflections of ourselves." - Ken Goldberg

Ed the engineer was a very busy person. He was in charge of the buildout of the new village, in charge of the energy distribution and in charge of maintaining a communications link to the mother ship.

So far they had placed multiple habitats and

temporary laboratories near a cleared area on the surface of the planet. Most of the buildings were simple structures and not strong enough for any intense winds or unexpected storms they might encounter. So far they had been safe and the mother ship had not detected any severe weather anywhere on the planet. There was however, a significant emphasis on building more permanent, stronger structures. Ed started the process with a 3D printer using indigenous materials, sometimes melted with lasers. He placed a robotic arm in the middle of a proposed building then programming it with a desired layout. The arm worked all hours of the day and night to place bits of building concrete along walls, floors and eventually roofs. Once complete the building was strong enough to last 100 years. The arm was then dismantled and moved to another spot to repeat the process. The building "owners" chose the plans and modified as necessary; once the process was initiated it only took a few days to complete. Overall the village would take a few months to complete but not knowing what the various seasons or possible seismic activity would be like, they worked with alacrity.

Ed's daily routine consisted of monitoring the building activities remotely (or on scene if necessary) then designing the electrical buildout to run the village followed by making sure the comm team was effectively transferring data at the optimal rates as the mother ship flew overhead periodically.

The morning typically took up the first task, then the design activities for the electrical buildout took the middle part of the day. After reviewing design plans, Ed had to deal with where to optimally place the solar arrays, the wind generators if needed and the any geo-thermal stations to round out the generation side of the designs. This planet had plenty of sun so the photovoltaics would dominate the input. They had a team of geologists who had been taking day trips out to various points of the compass to look for geothermal vents or volcanic activity; they had, at least at this point, not found anything of consequence. They sampled the earth at various levels and examined the striations along mountainous exposures. The data was all telemetered or recorded for later analysis. Every day as they returned the data was placed in a large data base and slowly a picture of the history of the planet emerged and was compared to the data sets provided by the astronomers. Again, the history told a story of technology followed by pollution followed by healing. What was curious was the physical absence of life at a stage that could produce what they were finding. Another curious detail was

161

that the technological cycle had taken place a very long time ago. Did this mean that the progenitors of these technologies had left? Or were they present but hidden?

These mysteries added to the discoveries of the astronomers and made for great lunch and dinner conversations. For now, however Ed needed to gather data, which would helpful in the discovery of the secrets on this planet.

He continued with his energy work by placing fiber optic cables in the ground, they carried both energy and data for all of their needs. Power from the solar arrays and wind generators activated CO_2 lasers that pumped high intensity light down the fiber optics to the rest of the buildings and residences in the village. Receptors there converted the light energy to electricity and power their equipment and lights. Data was also present on the fibers that connected every computational node together as a collective intelligence. A failure in any unit was backed up by the others. Deep AI had been employed to augment the pioneers' needs. Some of the people had cranial implants that allowed them to access the web, which connected to all the systems on the planet as well as in orbit. This came in handy when information was needed, however the background noise was worse than tinnitus. And of course, back on Earth, hackers had found ways to listen to your thoughts, the ultimate invasion of privacy.

Robots dug the trenches for the fiber optic cables and did all of the other dirty work. Ed monitored a group of them that had been instructed to do this work. If there were any problems, the robot would stop and await new instructions, which Ed provided. Robots also fed the 3D building printers and dug the foundations. All people had to do was be patient and wait until their dwellings or laboratories were complete before moving in and starting their tasks. Several robots had been sent out to be sentries and gather information about the planet. None of them were close the level of sophistication of Frank, and as per instruction, none of them were searching for him either.

Most of the robots were servant models and HL (Hard Labor) models, chosen to replace humans who once performed the same chores. Back on Earth, those humans were left in squalor until the right politics took hold and re-educated them into useful roles. Now it seems a way of life and few people remember when humans performed chores at that level. In fact, life has changed significantly since the dawn of the robot age and the achievement of the singularity. People in general are left to design, program and study their world. It is rare to find anyone who does not own a robot, even if it's an obsolete model. They are all still valuable tools no matter if you're a farmer, engineer or scientist. As far as what was needed on the new planet, robots were indispensable. They work constantly and guard as well as build. So far they have not sent out any alarms about intruders and have been for the most part, digging and building.

The transition through the singularity was a bit more complicated than getting used to robots. This happened decades ago and has produced conflicts and super beings as well as great strides in human progress. The point where artificial intelligence was more capable that humans' intelligence initially caused great stress on the humans. They knew that the AI systems could and would design and program much more efficiently than humans and with Moore's law still valid, it would not take long for the AI systems to leave human intellect in the dust. The first indications of this growth occurred when the systems were allowed to program themselves, soon a new language was produced that was much faster in terms of execution time than anyone had seen. Many new commands were introduced that produced much better results. Big data was used to compliment the new languages and soon, new computer topologies were requested by the AI systems.

These were built which again boosted their capabilities. The new combination of hardware and software were distributed amongst the available nodes and then into robots. Frank was a product of the 11th generation and had capabilities no one knew about. He was chosen for the trip to make sure the explorers had the best chance of success. Because he thought at 20 GHz, no human could keep up with his ability to make decisions and more importantly no human knew his motivations. Of course he would do as requested but by what means only he was privy.

The computer systems onboard Gaea also had deeply rooted AI algorithms, again to give the best chance of success. Frank was connected wirelessly and would always know exactly what was going on with the ship. He in fact chose to be a waiter at their cafeteria to both communicate and understand the moment to moment operations of the ship with the crew members. It turns out it did not matter where he chose to work as his control could be implemented anywhere.

Now Frank was gone, Ed continued to wonder what he was doing but had been shut down several times by the executive council when he asked questions. Ed felt that he was ultimately responsible for the safety of the explorers on the surface of the planet and also felt he needed to know what all of the team members were doing, be they human or android. So he deployed a swarm of drones under the pretense of survey work and perimeter security. But he also had a subroutine built into their search commands that would report any sighting of Frank. Some of these drones flew very high and very silently, others flew low and fast to get to trouble spots very quickly.

These drones flew almost all of the time, the smaller ones returning periodically for charging. The high altitude drones rarely returned as they were solar powered. The data they provided was ported into the main control center of the newly formed village. Ed had provided instructions to the technicians to have any data about Frank separated from the uplink telemetry to the mother ship. If any thing triggered a "Frank" alert, it had to set aside and Ed immediately notified. In fact for security the name Frank was changed to Sam, after one of the technicians. For several weeks after their flights were initiated, the drone swarm reported no sightings of anything fitting the description of Frank. As they continued, they flew farther and farther away from the base camp. As they did the time to cover the vast expanses of the land increased significantly. Finding a single android, who probably was in hiding, would take a long time. Ed however was satisfied with this reality as at least he knew that Frank was not near them now. Although not worried about Frank, Ed was still concerned about his erratic behavior and the strange commands from the executives on the mother ship.

Work continued at a serious pace on the ground; more and more people were transferring down from Gaea and filling out the village. Ed was the de-facto leader as most of the work required engineering. Within several more weeks, the village was self sufficient, with more than enough power for any equipment. Plumbing was complete, water distribution efforts were winding down and many permanent structures had been built. The 3D machines doing the building could work without breaks and were finishing houses within a few days now.

Ed spent most his time inside the command building monitoring the activity of both people and robots. He advised the others aboard the mother ship that they could come down at their leisure as their was plenty of space for them and enough knowledge about the planet to make the m feel comfortable and safe.

Flying over the New World

"Flying was a very tangible freedom. In those days, it was beauty, adventure, discovery – the epitome of breaking into new worlds." - Anne Morrow Lindbergh

Rudy was very busy, he shuttled people and equipment to and from the mother ship almost constantly and got to the point that he recognized geologic features from orbit and could transfer down to a smooth landing without the use of maps. The flying was good but the days long. Because of his attraction to Camomile, he adjusted his schedule so that he had time on the ground near lunchtime and after the day was complete. He stayed on the ground for the most part during the evenings and stayed on Gaea only when his shuttle needed maintenance or there was a particularly tricky load to bring down.

The days were long but productive; within a few weeks he had actually flown hundreds of thousands of pounds of cargo from the mother ship to the colony. The autopilot on the mother ship could actually detect the change in mass and had to make minor changes in the station keeping software. This would continue until approximately one third of the station mass was on the ground, which would take a few months. Rudy did not have to do all of the flying as there were other pilots, just not as senior. They also had drones which could do some of the work but were not able to carry the large loads the shuttle could.

Rudy was also in charge of the drone fleet. He had to set up the operations on the ground to coordinate the drone flights to be used for reconnaissance, exploration and security. For the most part these flights were autonomous and did not require human control. For instance, a drone would be programed to survey a certain area, it would take off, keep itself at a safe altitude and commence photography and air sampling. Several of the drones had hyper-spectral imagers which could see below the canopy of the forests as well as heat signatures. A few of the drones were more like relay stations, soaring to high altitudes and orbiting in one particular spot for days. These drones relayed messages from the lower altitude drones as well as survey parties on the planet's surface. More accurately called a constellation, these drone swarms were in place most of the time and vital to communications, safety and research.

A long time ago, Rudy had become a pilot, then instructor; adding all the way, numerous licenses and sign-offs to allow him to fly just about anything. He flew gliders, helicopters and sea planes while back on Earth and came to find being in the air an effortless endeavor. Flying does require great skill, and he had become a 1% of the 1% of the 1% in terms of capabilities. Naturally he applied to become a pilot for the planetary flight and after much success became the chief pilot of Gaea. Few people could override the commander, but Rudy could if there was imminent danger. There were a few incidents during their long voyage to this new world and Rudy stepped forward when he had to to make sure everyone was safe. Although his right, the commander did not like to relinquish his authority, even for a second. This did not endear him to Rudy but even he knew he lacked the skill set to accurately move a million ton spaceship at terrific speeds with swan like grace. Rudy could feel the heat from the commander but ignored it; he had a job to do.

Now on the ground, he was quite busy coordinating many flights a day including cargo trips to the mother ship. The thought of the commander and what he was doing was far from his mind. Closer to home however were his thoughts of Camomile, he was attracted to her and certainly wanted to take the next steps. The attraction started a long time ago when he first saw her from a distance. One of those waves of energy, maybe an aura, emanated from her even from a distance. She detected his gaze and looked right at him for a fleeting moment, then back again for another view. Of the thousands of people they both had seen over the years, they were attracted to each other instantly. One always wonders how this works in reality. Psychologists think about this phenomena and come up with theories but the reality seems to be how we project ourselves in the real world, where we are personally and maybe the position of the stars. In other words, it is not an exact science but something is happening.

He saw her quickly, they locked eyes and quickly he was trying to figure out a way to get to meet her. Considering he had no idea where she worked or what she did for fun, this quest had a very low probability of success. What he did not know, what that she was a scientist who had been assigned to the flight of Gaea and would be close at hand for many years.

Their next encounter took place on board the ship, as they passed in one of the corridors. They quickly locked eyes again and hesitated for a moment, long enough for Rudy to say "hello." She returned the greeting but had to move on with the group she was with. She did however glance back after a few moments to get another look at the pilot. He was still stopped in place and watching her walk away. He smiled instinctively at her second look. This meant a lot to him for obvious and maybe not so obvious reasons. He certainly wanted to find out more about her, but considering everyones' work load, this was not going to be easy.

Both of them seemed to be in a position to find someone, to fill a personal gap. Beyond that there was the aura they had for each other; unexplored, possibly dangerous but nonetheless needing exploration. Animals are like that, with attractions that cannot be easily explained. And here they were, with the distance increasing between them as they used all of their senses to find out who the other one was.

Rudy remembered the incident in detail, as did she. For now though, as the image was starting to fade, he walked into the command area and had to reset his brain to fly the ship. He was just coming up to speed at this time, when the ship had not left Earth's orbit. It was imperative that he concentrate and leave the images of her for later retrieval.

His next opportunity came during one particular dinner time when he could sit down and talk with her; she was still quite exciting and he again wanted to keep exploring. They talked for a while, then the dinner came to a natural end. They promised to find a way to meet again. He got very busy soon after that as the ship needed constant guidance and care. This had to come first. Sleeping on an airplane going across the ocean is not really sleeping if you are one of the pilots and Rudy felt the same way flying through space. There were course adjustments, most planned but some not, that had to be done carefully. There were hazards to navigation in space as well, especially going so fast. So although he might not be flying, he was always a short distance away in case they needed the best at the controls.

They had several radars and several lidars all at different frequencies probing the space ahead. Most obstacles were detected well in advance of any danger, but every once in a while, a lone rock or chunk of ice was detected very close to the ship, they had to change direction quickly or shoot it down or both. An infrared radar system was devised to both "skin paint" the object and heat it up to make it glow. Lasers were used for this application as they were quite powerful in this part of the electromagnetic spectrum. Finally the lasers could be used to ignite the offending rock.

In reality, they only had a few close calls during their long voyage. Most of the course corrections were not due to getting around space debris but adjusting for the changing positions of the star system they were headed for. The changing gravitational fields in outer space cause apparent changes in star positions. Although minor corrections were required the autopilots were always controlled by the telescopes pointed in the direction of their destination. Rudy watched the corrections as a way of telling the magnitude of the course changes and any unusual fields they were traveling through.

Back on land now, Rudy found himself busy yet

again but with a difference. He felt a bit more comfortable on land now. Mostly because the large part of his duties were complete and he now had a bit of time to relax. He also knew that Camomile was close and now that the stressful part of the journey was complete, he could make time to seek her out.

So, with no clear message about the intentions of the commander, Rudy started to etch out his future on land. His flying duties kept him busy during the day but only eight hours or less recently. Off duty he decided to follow his passions and build a small plane to explore the new countryside on his own. He chose an electric motor for propulsion, a spare from the drones. Then he chose a design very much like the Cessna 172s that dominated flight instruction and site seeing so many years ago. Plans were still available and with the spare sheets of aluminum from the mother ship, he started to make this four passenger airplane in what became known as "the garage." As many of the colonists were finding spare time on their hands, their creative instincts came out and music, painting and pottery started to appear in the central area of the new town.

He spent hours every evening with laser cutters, 3D printers and welding systems to create the wings, fuselage and empennage of the plane. It had enhancements over the original of course, mostly done for convenience. These included fly by wire, automatic engine controls and modern navigation electronics. With advanced assembly techniques and a little help from some spare robots, his airplane took form quickly, in just a few weeks. Window assemblies were printed, paint was applied, systems were checked and a weight and balance calculations performed. The day came for a test flight in short order; Rudy was almost not prepared for it. He had built the machine, done all of the proper calculations and obtained all of the final sign offs from systems experts who understood what he was doing. Now, one crisp Saturday morning, he was in the garage looking at the aircraft and sensing that it wanted to escape gravity and chase some clouds. He looked at it for a while longer, started to slowly circle it as one would do with a pre-flight check. The paint still smelled a bit as did the oder of new grease and electrical connections. It was pristine now, and would never be again. He closed in and ran his hand along the fuselage, checking underneath for anything foreign. In the old days of 172 flying, the pilot would do the same, run his or her hands along the skin, shake the flight controls, look at the brakes, look underneath for oil and generally examine the instrument of

176

freedom to see if it was whole and capable of keeping him or her alive for at least an hour. Once the ritual was complete, then and only then could the pilot consider sitting in the front seat and coaxing the machine into the air. Rudy was getting close to that point now, he thought about all of the details of the construction, all of the questions he answered from the experts and his general condition psychologically and spiritually. Was it time?

It was. His mood changed to business like and finding a tow bar, placed the forks into the nose wheel steering slots. With an initial hefty pull, he coaxed the airplane to a slow roll, out the garage doors (really the hangar doors now) and onto the flat surface that lead to the drone runway. Once outside he pulled the plane in an arc to keep the prop wash during ground testing away from any houses or people. He stopped the roll and removed the tow bar. This was left on the ground underneath the left wing for when he returned and had to tow it back into the hangar.

Rudy looked up at the sky for a simple weather check. The details of the forecasts were fresh in his mind and the reports from the drones indicated smooth air and light breezes. He smiled at the thought, having fought h is way through many storms, wind shears and serious cross winds. Today was perfect.

Opening up the left hand door, Rudy found the latest charts of the area including satellite images showing the terrain. He had been studying this for quite a while to get a sense of the area around the colonists. In particular he looked for potential landing areas in case of anything going wrong. He pulled himself in and put on his seat belt first. Then he pulled the check list out of its holder and using his thumb as a guide, started down the list of tasks to ready the plane for take off. The trim was set, the battery voltages checked, the navigation instruments initialized. Soon his list was complete and he was ready to start the engine. The door was closed, final switches set and he moved the throttle to the idle setting. As he did so, the plane's nose dipped a bit in response to prop's airflow going over the tail. This felt completely normal, especially for a 172. Next he examined the gauges for proper indications and advanced the throttle to initiate movement. He tested the brakes after about 10 feet of roll. They worked perfectly. Now the nose wheel steering, again perfect. The sense of normal was starting to seep into his brain. He taxied about 30 yards and came to a stop on the taxiway for the main runway. Again he looked at all of his instruments for proper behavior and advanced the throttle to full power to make sure the plane was ready and capable for take off. He had done this several times before the aircraft was completed. As the electric motor system was very simple, no problems were ever observed and now after the latest test, he felt confident that we would not encounter any problems during flight.

Pulling the throttle back, he paused to make sure every detail had been taken care of. Just for a final test he performed the "CIGARS" test which was a simplified way of seeing if the aircraft was ready to fly. Controls, Instruments, Gas (now battery status), attitude, radios and safety. All was in order and he looked forward while advancing the throttle to move the plane to the take off point of the runway. Calling on the radio he announced his intentions for take off and staying in the pattern for some initial flight handling tests. Although the drone airport did not have any control tower, there were people listening on the channel who knew Rudy, they responded with wishes of good luck and safe flying. Rudy acknowledged them and knew that his radios work fine and as the transmissions would be recorded, he could give them a running dialogue of his impressions of the flying characteristics of the new machine which he had named 'Capella One."

"Colony area traffic, this is Capella One taxiing for takeoff, runway zero niner"

He advanced the throttle and moved the aircraft to the starting position at the end of the runway. Stepping on both brakes, he brought it to a stop. One final time, he checked the gauges, completed his take off check list, started the event recorder, turned on the strobes and transponder.

Looking through the windshield, he announced again:

"Colony area traffic, Capella One is on the roll for take off, straight out departure."

"Have a great flight, came a voice over the radio." Rudy was not expecting anything like this and his only reaction was to smile.

Another voice, "Keep her head up."

Rudy was getting busy now with the acceleration and up coming rotation speed. He was only able to respond with one word.

"Roger."

Acceleration was brisk, much better than a four banger Cessna of old. He realized he was going to blow right through the 55 Knot rotation bug so he instinctively applied a little back pressure on the yoke. Within a second or two the craft jumped into the air and continued accelerating. His choice now was to lower the nose and pull the throttle back or raise the nose and get more altitude without changing anything. As everything was okay at this setting and altitude is your friend, he chose the latter course and pulled up the nose to best climb speed. Considering the power of the electric motor and the smoothness of the design, his nose attitude was over 40 degrees, much like a jet fighter. Things were happening very quickly as this plane was sprinting for the stars. Rudy had to slow down and get back to a more normal attitude.

"You okay," came a voice of the radio, "You took off like a Viking missile."

Rudy could breath a bit now as he passed 2,000 feet above ground.

"Yeah, we are fine. This bird is a bit spritely."

"No shit, Orville. You look like you are flying through butter with a very hot knife."

"I am bringing the power back now, the nose attitude almost hit 45 degrees, still accelerating. Quite a ride. I guess it will fly."

"Yep, looks like it's flying like an angel from here, what are your intentions Capella One?"

"We are going to slow down to check out here flying characteristics at different speeds then enter the pattern from the North for some landings and take offs."

"Good deal, Capella. Oh and by the way, we got a call from the Mother ship, wondering what was going on."

"The commander upset?"

"No one has seen the commander or that stupid robot for weeks, so I guess that is what we call a tacit approval."

"Roger that. So I am about the get a little busy here, talk to you when I get on the ground."

"Understood, we are following you with radar and telemetry. Let us know if you need anything, we will continue monitoring this channel."

"Ok, thank you. Capella One remaining on channel."

Rudy slowed the plane down by changing the throttle setting from 300 Kw to 100 Kw. The plane slowed down reluctantly and settled at 120 knots indicated. "Amazing," thought Rudy. His simulations of the performance had these speeds at the upper end of theoretical. Because he spent so much time in putting together a slippery fuselage, his speeds were much better than he was expecting. "Could be a problem on landing," he thought again.

With such a slippery plane, landing could be difficult because it simply does not want to stop flying. Rudy had experience with a few planes like this, even a 172 many years ago. He was doing some stalls and found that this particular plane would not stall, once down to very low airspeeds, it would just mush through the air and not break the nose over like a normal stall. He could actually fly this machine at 30 knots by keeping his rudders active.

Now however, he could only hope that the flaps would "dirty up" the plane enough to let it land within a reasonable distance.

Rudy brought the throttle up a bit to 150 Kw and saw the increase in airspeed, another 15 knots, which was amazing. He turned for home and set himself up to enter the traffic pattern at a 45 degree angle, just like his flight instructor so many years ago taught him. He dropped the nose a bit, increasing speed yet again and aimed for 1,000 feet above the airport for pattern height. Doing so while instinctively pulling the throttle back to keep his speed in check.

Once he was about a kilometer from the runway at the correct altitude, he looked around for other traffic, then banked right to enter the traffic pattern.

"Capella One is entering the traffic pattern, left down wind. We will do several landings and take offs, other traffic please advise intentions and positions."

He was on automatic now and did not think that there was no traffic at all flying within 20 miles of him. His focus was intent on the landing and old habits simply bubbled up to the surface.

The recommended speed in the pattern was 70 knots, which he intended on keeping as he descended from the pattern, though base leg to final. Across the fence he intended on keeping 65 knots which would be plenty safe for an airplane that could certainly fly at 50. Across from the numbers on the runway he added a single notch of flaps to see if they performed properly. Normally the first notch or 10 degrees would add more drag than lift. He observed that in fact the plane was now descending at about 300 feet per minute, a little low but understandable considering the smooth design. He planned to extend his legs to make sure each configuration change was stable. The air was smooth and the view was stunning, he smiled once again.

Now a left turn to base leg and another notch of flaps. The transition was smooth without any need for trim adjustment. Currently there was equal drag increase with lift increase. The plane kept its proper speed by pushing the nose over a little bit. All was normal so far. Rudy looked out the left window and considering the winds and his position, chose the right moment to take the final left hand turn to final. The plane lined up with the runway, was perfectly in trim and for a moment, Rudy took his hands off of the yoke to make sure everything was balanced. It was and he responded with another smile. This plane actually flew incredibly well with great stability and responsiveness.

Now on final, he waited until the proper moment to add the last notch of flaps, bring them to 30 degrees now on the trailing edges of the wings. There was a small increase in noise as the drag increased a bit more and the lift increased significantly. Still, all was stable, the nose went down a small amount to keep the speed up. Once over the fence (approaching the runway threshold in pilot's terms) he released a bit of forward yoke pressure to allow the nose to rise and the airspeed to drift to the required 65 knots landing speed. He trimmed up a bit more and could fly the aircraft easily with his thumb and index finder. The world slowed down as he crossed the numbers at an altitude of about 10 feet. The plane seemed to know what to do next as it continued to descend to about three feet then sit down on the runway. The main wheels kissed the surface, the nose wheel hesitated for a second or two then gently lowered to touch the center stripe.

"Great approach and landing," came a voice from the radio.

"Yeah, that felt really good," said Rudy. "I am going to taxi back and take off for another landing, but that was very stable."

"Understood, Capella One."

Rudy taxied the plane back to the take off point and again added throttle, accelerated, flew into the air quickly and entered the pattern for another landing. This time he would use less flaps and try to slip (fly sideways) the aircraft down as a method of altitude control. The aircraft flew true to its design and felt great. He touched down with a faint squeak; not satisfied he again rose into the air and across from the numbers on downwind, he pulled the power completely on the engine and practiced a loss of engine maneuver. Again, everything felt great. He did a full stop landing and taxied back to the hangar to examine the plane for any abnormal stresses or leaks.

Once he shut the systems down and the electronic fans whined down to silence, he surveyed the instruments and downloaded all of the engineering data for examination. Most of the gritty details of the test flight would be found here. Although its great to fly a machine for the first time and practice some maneuvers, the data holds a lot of clues as to the quality of the airplane. He waited for the download to complete and then took the memory chip and placed it in his pocket. Looking around the cabin of the plane, he made sure everything was cleaned up and opened the door to exit. Once outside he did a final check then crossed the seat belts as his instructor had taught him so many years ago. He smiled at the thought.

Rudy placed chocks around the landing gear after his inspection and with one final glance at his new toy, walked away and into his lab to review the data. It was cooler inside and Rudy had that afterglow from a well executed flight plan leading to a safe arrival feeling. Again he smiled, walked towards the lab bench where the design computers were and plugged in his memory chip. The data from the flight was compared to the simulations he performed while designing the aircraft. Numerous graphs appeared on the screens comparing real to mathematically derived data. Every sim just about perfectly matched the measurements. This meant the design was good and that the sims were accurate as well, so Rudy could extrapolate what performance he could expect under extreme conditions without stressing the plane.

Eventually, after several more test flights and ringing out, Rudy felt comfortable enough to take a passenger for a ride. He knew who he wanted but had to find a way to ask her.

After work one day he ventured to the mess hall for dinner and chanced upon Camomile sitting by her self at a table by the window. After a brief pause he decided he had nothing to lose but his pride and walked over to greet her.

"Hello Camomile, how are you?"

"Great, good to see you Rudy. Please sit down; we haven't talked in a long time."

Rudy smiled the smile of a win and sat down. He took his plates off of the tray and arranged them neatly. Then with a sip of his tea asked:

"How are the stars these days?"

"They are doing great, thank you. So far they are staying put, which is a good thing. It's much easier to read them when they are not moving as they did when we came over here."

"I understand completely, Camomile. It's nice not to worry about trajectories and speed as well," Rudy said smiling faintly.

"I'll bet."

A pause while they both though of more to say.

"Um, Camomile, I was wondering if you would like to take a short flight in my new plane? Maybe tomorrow or Sunday if you're free."

"Oh, I would love to Rudy. I've heard about your flying machine and it seems safe enough," she said smiling.

"Great, that's great. Thank you, I was hoping you would like to do that. We can go over the forest and rivers here; they are quite beautiful."

"Sounds like fun, when should I come over to the hangar?"

"How about ten tomorrow?"

"Perfect, I will bring a camera."

Rudy smiled at yet another win and started to work on his dinner. She did as well and at some point they started to talk about other things and the people they work with. They were both happy and looking forward to the next day.

After dinner he walked her home and unexpectedly received a quick kiss right before Camomile went into her quarters. His last image of her was a nice smile as the door shut.

It was evening now and somehow it was a perfect day, with perfect weather and a perfect outlook on life. Rudy walked home with a smile and a sense of greatness. He took in several deep breathes of the clean sweet air and remembered what the older people on Earth talked about before pollution forced most people to wear filter masks. This lead him to think about the short sightedness of the politicians and other people in positions of power and how they had selfishly kept the atmospheric scientists and ecologists from getting the truth to the populations about the directions they were heading. Rudy now thought about one of the reasons he and his fellow explorers were sent out into space, to find an alternative to living with greed and selfishness. The truth hit hard once the environment on Earth collapsed and the one thing you should never mess with (Mother Nature) took over with meteorological violence to snuff out the problems and start over. Billions of lives were lost, most of the animals and insects were wiped out and the only real winners in the catastrophe were algaes and pond scums reminiscent of the very early epochs of Earth's existence.

Now however he knew he was lucky in so many ways. He had admirable skills, an admirable home and now an admirable future.   Camomile represented the culmination of much of his life in terms of the end game or place he wanted to be now and in the future.

Soon he found himself back home and felt that he had no idea where he was walking during the journey from her doorstep. His mind had been filled with many thoughts and warm feelings. He entered his living quarters, sat down and started looking at the forecast for the flight. Weather on this planet was mild and very predictable, so he only had to do a quick check of the long range forecast and the current conditions. The trend of the barometric pressure was very minor, unlike that on Earth when things started to go crazy. Again he smiled at his place in life; lucky to be were he was.

He caught up on some reading and then went to sleep to dream a gentle dream.

The next morning he fell out of bed refreshed and a bit earlier than normal. He ate breakfast, rechecked the weather and got ready to go to the airport.

While walking there he looked at the clouds and kept track of the wind. The temperature was just like it was for the last several days, mild. Once at the airport he made his way to the hangar and opened the large door, exposing his airplane to early sunlight. He did his normal walk around and pre-flight checks then did them again in reverse order to make sure he did not miss anything. A self check of the electronic systems in the plane (and they were comprehensive) showed no issues or concerns.

The plane was fine so there was not much more to do but wait for Camomile, he pulled a chair up in front of the plane and sat down to relax until she arrived.

Not long after he got comfortable, Camomile showed up. In fact she was early, eager to get up in the air and have fun with Rudy.

He smiled at her arrival.

"Good morning," he said.

"And a good morning to you as well, Rudy. Is the airplane in good shape?"

"I think so and it thinks so."

"Great! Let's get some air!"

They pulled the airplane out of the hangar far enough to keep the prop wash from blowing dirt in to it. They got in and buckled up. Looking at Camomile for a quick second, Rudy then pulled out the check list and started going over every line item, keeping his thumb on the line as a place keeper so as not to miss anything. He reviewed each item, set the switches properly, called "Clear Prop!" out of the window and set the engine to idle mode. He then checked all of the instrumentation for proper indication, looked both left and right for traffic and started to taxi to the active runway. On his way, he pressed the microphone button and spoke:

"Village area traffic, Cessna November zero zero one alpha taking the active runway zero niner; any local traffic please advise position and intentions."

Of course he heard nothing and did not expect to hear anything. What he did expect was to have the drone pilots hear him and know what his intentions were. He spoke again after waiting several seconds.

"Village area traffic, Cessna November zero zero one alpha rolling runway zero niner for a straight out departure, followed by a turn to the North at one thousand feet."

He advanced the throttle, which pressed them both back in their seats and waited for the quick arrival of rotation speed.

Pulling back slightly, the weight on the nose wheel was removed and the wings started to create lift. In a few more seconds, this lift overcame the weight of the aircraft and it levitated into the air, the best kind of take off. The ground just fell away from them as he reached forward to set the trim wheel to the proper position to relieve any pressure on the control yoke. He could now fly with his thumb and finger tip.

The air was smooth and cool today and a few clouds could be seen miles away. The overwhelming sensations was the air was pure and unpolluted; no haze or brown cloud to contend with. Rudy took his hand away from the control yolk, which did not produce any change in attitude. Camomile noticed this and remarked:

"Nice, smooth air, huh?"

"Yeah, it's great up here. Most days are like this unless storms are in the vicinity. Nice laminar air flow and the boundary layer is usually very low."

"It's so clear up here!"

"Yep, would you like to fly?"

"Sure, I actually have my pilot's license but it's been a while so don't go far."

"Oh I won't, maybe just into the back seat to take a nap; you're doing great. Climb and maintain three thousand feet please."

"You got it."

They continued to rise until they reached the target altitude. She reached over and adjusted the trim wheel once they got there and the plane seemed motionless. There are times in such smooth air that pilots get the clear sensation that they could just open the door and step outside, even though they are screaming through the air at the time. Good headsets get rid of the noise and the lack of motion or vibration in smooth air combine for a very peaceful sensation. On Earth this does not happen very often, the last time Rudy experienced it was just after a snow storm, at night with a full moon. The sensation was very strong then. It felt like the Earth was moving and he was stationary.

Here however, the weather was generally very good, mostly calm with consistent long range forecast accuracy. At some point during the initial portions of the flight, the two pilots smiled.

Rudy smiled the most as he felt great spending time with Camomile and it was a great stroke of luck that she was also a pilot and therefore enjoyed flying. After a few minutes Rudy spoke.

"This plane flies like a homesick angel, doesn't it?"

"Yes, its very stable and the control harmony is great. Is this fly by wire?"

"Not really, just very well balanced. The auto pilot however is very sophisticated and uses machine learning to make fine adjustments. It's capable of complete autonomy from take off to landing, even through bad weather."

"Nice."

"Yeah, it will come in handy whenever we have challenging conditions."

"Have you tried it yet?"

"No, just simulations. The weather here is pretty stable and while testing I didn't want to take too many risks."

"But isn't one test worth a thousand simulations?"

Rudy looked back at her with a bit of alarm in his face.

"I tell you what, when we get a thunderstorm, I will pick you up and we can do the cowboy thing, how does that sound?"

"Perfect," she said with a smirk.

They continued exploring the countryside for another 45 minutes or so. She took pictures and he deftly maneuvered the plane to get the best look angles for her. They enjoyed every moment of the experience but all too soon, it was time to head back.

"Shall we return to the barn?"

"I guess, if we have to. This has been great."

"Yes it has, glad you liked it. You're welcome to come up any time."

"Ok, thanks. I'd love to do this again," she said smiling and looking at him for a little bit longer than usual.

"Good, me too. Okay, you have the controls, lets go ahead and take a heading of zero three zero and descend to two thousand."

"Zero three zero and two thousand."

She lowered the nose while taking a shallow left turn toward the assigned heading, anyone who would have been flying with them would have hardly noticed the change. They flew on in silence for several more minutes, drinking in the beautiful scenery and fun first date.

"Dinner?" She asked.

"Absolutely, you get to pick."

"Oh, so many options, so little time. How about the commissary?"

"Hmmm, I haven't been there since.....this morning."

"Good, I will meet you there at 7:00 this evening."

"I'm looking forward to it," said Rudy with a sincere smile.

"You want to land it?" asked Rudy

"Sure, I have the field in sight. How about a left downwind at 70 knots?"

"Perfect, then over the fence at 65."

"You got it."

She lowered the nose a bit more as they got closer to enter in the pattern, he made the appropriate announcements on the radio while she slowed it down to approach speeds. Soon they were taking a left turn to enter base leg, then final. She slowed it down a bit more and performed a perfect landing.

"Grease."

"Thank you, it's been a while."

"Well that was very nicely done, maybe a flight or two more and you will be checked out for solo."

"Great, thanks, I would like that," she said with a broad smile.

They taxied up to the hangar, shut the plane down, got out and pushed it back in to complete a successful first date. Both were happy, and both were looking forward to a relaxed evening at the commissary.

Their relationship evolved from this very moment into a comfortable loving existence on the new planet. Years later they would remember their first flight together with warmth.

Life with the Animals

"There are things that the horse did for me that a human couldn't have done." - Buck Brannaman

Buck however was working hard. He had multiple animals to bring down to the surface. This was no easy task as some of the species were docile and easy to herd. Others like the horses, could get anxious and cause problems. Initially he brought the easy ones down first, got them situated in a pen and started introducing new foods to them. The vegetation on the planet was very similar to that on Earth.

He was also in charge of the husbandry center where frozen embryos were allowed to grow in a synthetic womb to be introduced into the animal population once fully grown. An analysis had been made of the local animals and computer simulations of the impact of new animals in a world where they had no evolutionary background. Only a few Earth species would be allowed to intermix as it turned out, one per year. The consequences were too great. Buck's farm however would be large, open and protected. People would come and see his animals grazing and living good lives. The only consequences were population control until many generations in the future when someone there would be able to make an informed choice about introducing more of the animals to the planet.

For now he had to ferry the horses, pigs and cattle to the ground; this usually meant he would be with them during the transition to keep them calm.

Buck had an amazing gift of calmness that everyone and every animal was aware of. He realized that all animals communicated, had feelings and moods. There were times when your best horse companion needed to be alone. There were other times when the animals needed attention or just wanted to be near you. Buck knew this language and as he chose which species would be transported next, he watched them and talked to them. The horses for instance knew something was going on; they had spent so many months in a technical world, certainly not home on a ranch. They knew they were being transported and that because Buck was there, they would be safe. Upon arrival he walked amongst them after his normal feeding time and let them know that the following day, they would be moved into a small ship (like a horse trailer) and taken down to the surface. They sensed his meaning and they could smell the new planet on him after he started visiting the ground to make preparations. During this period, they gathered around him to sense all of the aromas he was bring back, which he was not aware of. Horses can have smell sensitivities as good as the best dogs; heir hearing and eyesight are very acute as well. So they see and feel more than what Buck is trying to communicate to them. They sensed consistency, safety and different yet aromatic grasses waiting for them. So when the day came for them to follow him through the hallways to the transfer shuttle, they walked closely behind him in good moods. He guided them one by one into the awaiting stalls and gave each a sedative. The trip would include being weightless for a while which would definitely be a foreign sensation for them. It would feel like being in water up to their necks, just without the water. Inside the shuttle, there were projectors depicting an ocean around them; that plus the tranquilizers kept the animals calm. They were tied down with flexible cords to keep them in place yet give them the freedom to move.

The trip from mother ship to ground took less than an hour with a weightless period of around 30 minutes. Buck sat with the animals and TV screens. He looked into their eyes to make sure they were okay. When the initial sensations of zero gravity came on he started talking to them, which was a good distraction. Within a few minutes they knew they would be okay and settled into the ride. Once gravity returned some felt as though they had been taken from a fun place. You could tell by the expressions on their faces. But ultimately, they were looking forward to what was producing the new smells and different activities of the crew. Upon landing the horses looked out the ship's portholes at the new light from a sun much like the one they left so long ago. Soon the air inside of the shuttles was equalized with the air outside, bringing in the new smells.

Their ears went strait up and they started to move around in their stalls in anticipation of the new world.

Upon leaving the shuttle they looked around, smelled and listened. Buck took them off one by one and led them to a pasture, the size of which they had not seen in a very long time. Once all of the horses had been transferred they started to run and kick with happiness at their new home. The grass was good, there was clear water to drink and even mud to roll around in. Buck stood and watched for a long while and felt that now this whole trip was worth it. After quite a few minutes, he reluctantly left the pasture, closed the gate and while giving one last long look at his friends, went back to the shuttle to continue bringing the other animals down.

The thing about a farm is that all of the animals are aware of each other and do not like to see some of them taken away. There is a feeling of danger that accompanies the departure of those who you trust. Buck knew this and had to continue the shuttle trips 12 hours a day until the bulk of the larger animals were down and situated with food and water. What was left was the smaller "critters" like squirrels, bats and birds. These came down in a multitude of travel cages and released into large fenced in cages much larger than what they had experienced for the last many months. Even their behavior was notable in that the animals knew there was a change coming, the bird song changed, the amount of activity in the other animals changed and they all noticed that their larger brothers and sisters had all left.

Soon, after several days of intense work, all of the animals were transferred to the new farm. All that was left was the frozen embryos and DNA samples. For now these would be stored as before, just on the new planet. Now Buck had to spend time watching the animals adapt to their new environment. Most did quickly but all sensed the presence of the other indigenous inhabitants. Buck watched closely and as expected curiosity of the indigenous overcame their fears and they started to gather around, sometimes during the day and sometimes during the night, to see their new neighbors. After a few weeks, life returned to normal for most of the curious however some stayed to become friends. Interestingly the indigenous birds spent a lot of time with the horses and cattle; they seemed to communicate with a language that spoke about stories in their past and hopes for their futures.

Buck took notes and when Peg was available, she joined him to help with the observations. She had many of Buck's skills and was able to interpret how the animals were doing based on their noises and movements. At one point, Buck asked her the appropriate question:

"Which do you like better Peg, animals or humans?"

"Animals."

"Why?"

"Because they are honest."

"True enough, I've always felt comfortable with them. I taught quite a few clinics, mainly on horse behavior and found that most of my work was training the owners, not the animals."

"I agree. I used to teach riding classes and found the same thing. I also did a lot of equine therapy classes and found that the horses would unlock the minds of the autistic, mentally disabled, and other tortured souls."

"Humans could learn so much by spending more time with animals; somehow their past induced them to kill them for their muscles, skins or tusks. We lost so many of our species on Earth the only way we could preserve them was to sample their DNA. Not all were sampled but we brought quite a few on our voyage. The issue is how to bring them back to life. It's an ethical question more than anything. If they mix with the animals already here, we only have a hint of what could happen. Our simulations indicate most animals would stay in their own specie lines but some could intermix and the creation of new species or even new viruses, that is not comforting."

"What is the near term plan?"

"We will keep the larger animals outside but fenced in wildlife management areas. We will control the populations to some degree. The smaller animals will live in very large penned in areas. Large enough so the individuals will think its infinite in size. Within a few years we will have enough data to make further decisions about intermixing the species with those outside. So far, it looks like there are similarities, like primates, invertebrates, vertebrates, fish, avian life, plant life, etc. The long term plan is to watch and study and be extremely patient. This has never been done before."

"Looks like you have job security then."

"For a long time, Peg," he said smiling.

After a week or so with all of the animals situated and adjusted to their new surroundings. Buck (with help from Peg) built a large pole barn with 20 stalls, several tack rooms, a feed room and large hallways. They placed rubber mats on the concrete floors of the halls then put cross ties up. This would be useful when they needed to keep a horse in place when they cleaned and clipped hooves. All of the stalls had dirt floors with lots of soft wood chips covering them. Each stall had a watering station and a place to put hay for the horses. The barn was surrounded by pens for the other animals with lean to covers in case of bad weather.

Once the barn was complete they started to build a home nearby to live in. The whole farm was on a large 150 acre plot which they managed on a daily basis. Just feeding the animals took many hours, moving the horses in and out of the barn also took a good amount of time. But all of this was ritualized, the animals knew exactly when certain events would take place. So did Buck and Peg. The daily routines were punctuated by periodic animal ops for the rest of the people in the village. They built a few wooden carriages and taught several of the horses how work as a team. The horses they chose for this were Percherons, which were large (18.5 hands) draft horses with very gentle personalities. Truly gentles giants, once you got to know them and have mutual trust, you could go anywhere with them. Once every other weekend or so, they would hitch up a couple of these horses and ride into town to give people rides or just let them spend time with the horses in a park. It was amazing what kind of reactions people displayed.

Most everyone is fascinated by horses, especially when they are calm. Some men are afraid of them and won't get within 10 meters, others are cautious. Little girls have no fear and run right up to them to give them a hug which the horses don't mind. Women have little fear and approach slowly wanting to give the horse respect and asking for acceptance. Not all of these behaviors are standard, just interesting to watch. Many times Buck or Peg would witness someone one (many times a young girl) fall in love with the horse and announce that their heart had been taken. It also seemed that young adults and middle aged people would somehow create a bond and transfer emotional energy back and forth with the animal. It's a matter of clear record that horses have been used very effectively as therapy aids. Many equine specialists say that "they are a mirror into your soul." Trite perhaps but non-the-less somewhat accurate. They are also honest. Both Buck and Peg tell people to watch a horse's ears as an indication of what they are feeling. If a horse pins it's ears back on its head it is angry and might bite. Normally the ears are like radars and move about to survey the surroundings. If they become alert to something the ears will stand straight up and focus in the direction of the noise. Peg also says she watches the eyes carefully as they are trying to communicate as well. If the horse is afraid, the eyes will pop out a bit and the demeanor will be nervous.

This would be a good time to calm the horse and try to understand what it is concerned about. Mostly though a horse becomes relaxed and trusting when a person does the same. So much so that they can rely on each other when there is a need. A good example is when someone is out riding late at night and cannot see very well, you can trust the horse which has better vision, hearing and smell than a human to take you home safely. Another example is when (and this happens with all animals) there is danger, there will be a reaction. For example if a stranger approaches and the person who knows the horse becomes uncomfortable, the horse will protect its friend. If the danger continues to be present, the horse will turn its back side toward the problem and could very quickly kick it to pieces.

That being said, Buck turned to more important things. The most important task he needed to complete was to protect the animals from the humans; although they mean well, most do not give the beasts the respect they deserve. He formulated classes and visits that would help educate the PhDs and other highly educated to understand the simple truth of animal behavior is to leave them alone. Let them teach you, just like pre-school kids need to educate their teachers as to how best allow them to learn.

He designed walking trails and viewing areas for the colonists and their future offspring. Peg worked with him when she could and together they were able to protect and husband the animals.

Other's helped over the following years, helped with feeding and mucking (all important). Initially, they brought people in who they felt could commit themselves in terms of time and interest. They taught them how to feed, which would endear them to the hungry animals. They held classes on health, environment and the future placement of the animals in the wild.

Eventually, the animals and their human companions settled in over the next many years. The "farm" as it was referred to became that peaceful place to escape to when stresses in the outside world became too great. This was a mirror of what once was on Earth. Thus it became heaven, a vacation spot and the best place to hike.

Buck stayed with the animals of course over this period of time and became a fixture at the barn, all of the animals knew his patience, kindness and felt the safety of his presence.

One day, as he was out in the middle of one of the pastures working on a horse's bridle, Buck was incapacitated in one quiet moment with a heart attack. He fell to the ground and expired. The horses, cognizant of what had just happened, made a strange noise that most if not all of the other animals understood. They made their way to the place where Buck had fallen and gathered in a circle, heads down and silent. They bowed their heads. Other animals came as well and stood around the circle, much like a cloud of asteroids and planets around a sun. They all stood in silence, in reverence and in peace.

It took several hours for any human to realize that Buck was gone. Months afterwords, some people who were maybe overly sensitive said that they felt that something was wrong at that moment of the day. Something "cosmic" they said. Its hard to imagine what exactly they were talking about except to say that most people have these sensitivities.

Peg found him first, she had gone to the barn to tend to her horses, Andromeda and Capella. She had fed them grain, with a bit of flax seed for their coats. She had also brushed them down which they both enjoyed and generally spent time with them. Horses are very social and given the choice, will spend time with people who they like.

After the brushing she went into the hay stall and placed a bail in the wheelbarrow to take out to the horse's pasture.

During the brushings, she did notice that Andromeda and Capella were a bit low on energy, listless in fact. They did exactly what she wanted as she positioned them and fed them but something was off, she thought. As she brought back the bale of hay from around the barn, they pointed towards the pasture and doing so gave her a glimpse of what was happening in the main pasture. She saw a grouping of animals, many of which would not be near each other normally. Hunters and prey so to speak.

She dropped the wheelbarrow onto the ground and stared at the site. The animals surrounded something like a mound in the center, it was very hard to see. There were chickens, goats, deer, horses, cows, dogs, birds, squirrels and cats all surrounding this thing. Peg sensed that it was safe to move closer even though several of the animals could be mean, they showed no aggressiveness now. She opened the gate to the large pasture and started walking towards the mass of animals. Some of them noticed her coming but indicated that there was no danger in doing so. She walked well over 100 yards before she could start guessing as to what was going on. A few yards further, she froze with the realization that the mound was a person and even more chilling that the person could very well be Buck.

She called his name:

"Buck?"

"Buck, are you okay?"

No answer. She started to move quickly to find out if he was incapacitated or worse. As she did so the animals watched her and actually parted a path for her to go directly to the fallen Buck. She had never experienced this before, maybe in her dreams but never a real life show of high intelligence from the animals she had spent so much time with and thought she knew.

She got to the body and knelt down. The animals instinctively closed the gap to protect her.

"Buck?"

"Oh, Buck, please no..."

She put her hand on his face and its coldness told her the rest of the story. He had spoken to her recently about some "minor" chest pains. As he never complained about anything personal, this was a big admission. She urged him to see a doctor, he acquiesced and set up an appointment at some later date. He had "work to do" he said, and would see the doctor when he had a break. Peg worried a bit but Buck's calm demeanor allayed her fears and she knew these were his choices, not her's.

The body was without stress and maybe a faint

smile could be detected on Buck's face. After many minutes of full thought she looked up to see a hundred pairs of eyes on her telling her that this was just a passage not an end. Again, she noted the completely unusual behavior of the animals.

She spoke to them quietly, "He is going to a better place, and he is in no pain now." They all looked at her and waited. "I know that all of you sense when a person you love is in pain, I also know that all of you have experienced death, usually close to you here at the farm. We humans have less experience than you. We hide it sometimes by sending our loved ones to hospitals or hospices where others take care of the experiences we do not like to have. The animals continued to listen to her.

"Its okay now, we will take care of the body and grieve for our friend, just as you are doing now."

At this moment, most of the animals knew that a transition had been made, they started to move away and go back to the areas from which they came. Several remained, mostly horses but also a mule, a deer and several birds. Peg knew that this is what they wished and she had no problem with it. She looked at them each, right into their eyes and said:

"You can stay as long as you want, I need to tell the

others and will be right back."

Generally, everyone knows that animals do not understand the complex nuances of the spoken language. However few people understand that animals are mostly visual, they see the hand movements, the facial expressions, the walking style. They also sense moods, by in how people talk to them or the volume of the words or the pace of the delivery. They sense much more than we give them credit for. Peg knew this and simply let her sounds and movements deliver the message; the animals understood completely.

She walked away from the smaller grouping, out of the pasture and over to the barn where she could communicate what had happened to the others. Within minutes people started to stream over, Buck had a lot of friends. Most people left their work and many their homes to come to the farm and see Buck one last time. After her phone calls, Peg went back to the place where Buck's body remained. As she got closer she noticed that the same animals were there, they noticed her when she got a bit closer and again parted way to allow here in. She stopped however to look and try to understand what the animals were emoting. She soon realized that because Buck's life was lived amongst them more than people, they should have their wishes granted as to how to respect his life. What this means is that animals who live their lives out in the wild, will stay near a fallen friend or loved one until they have processed the emotions and filed the memories appropriately away. Peg knew that this meant the body should remain where it fell and become part of their world.

Others started to get to the barn and walk out to see Peg and the animals surrounding the body. The animals there sensed the onslaught of humans and all started to leave. Peg let them know she understood what they wanted:

"Don't worry, everything will be okay."

They acknowledged with a look and continued to leave well before the people got there. Before they did however, she took note of who had remained. Buck's favorite horses with one in particular, "Dusty," who was his constant companion. They had perfect trust for each other and each had the other save them from a catastrophe at some point in their lives. Because horses see much better at night, have much better olfactory sensors and can hear much better, Dusty had on several occasions took Buck home after a long night of trail riding. It would get to the point where Buck could no longer see the details of the ground and had to let Dusty take over navigation. He always did so perfectly. Buck on the other hand would always save Dusty from ignorant humans. Dusty's memory was perfect on this point and he retained images of people messing with him and Buck running over to chase them away.

People started to come over to see the body, including a doctor and nurse. They probed and measured, confirming he was indeed dead. Their instruments indicated that he had died of a massive cardiac arrest, one in which nothing could have been done. The doctor remarked that Buck must have known about the condition and had experienced quite a lot of acute pains.

"I wish he had come to see us in the clinic. We might not have been able to save him without a transplant, however we could have made him more comfortable."

Peg replied, "This was his way, he would have gladly given up weeks in a hospital for minutes with his animals."

"I understand and you're right, he would have. My daughters used to come here to see the horses, Buck had a way with the animals and humans that few of us share. You're the closest one with that gift, Peg. I guess this farm is yours now."

The other people present acknowledged that reality

and in that moment, Peg and the animals became one.

"What should we do with the remains," asked the nurse?

Peg answered, "the animals would prefer that he stays here, I suggest that we cover him with dirt and plant a nice tree over him."

"Okay, I think that is a great idea, Peg."

With that, the people who were present started to walk towards the barn to find shovels, rakes and wheelbarrows. Peg walked with them, mostly in silence and after finding the tractor, climbed up into the drivers seat, paused to think of the relevance of that move, started the engine and drove it to the burial site.

They worked for a little over an hour, making a very nice mound and surrounding area that looked both peaceful and respectful. During their work, quite a few of the animals returned, the horses pawed at the dirt and some of the dogs dug holes. All of this somewhat random activity was actually done in an attempt to help. Soon the burial was complete, all who were present paused for a minute in silence, each remembering a great human being and friend. Slowly the people started to go back to their homes and places of work. Peg of course stayed until everyone was gone, within the next day or two, she would plant a maple tree in the center of the memorial. She gathered the shovels and other tools and placed them in the bucket of the tractor. She then started it up and returned it to the protection of the barn. Once there, she unloaded the bucket, put away the tools and at one point turned and found Dusty right there with her. He had followed her into the barn and waited for her to complete her chores before he came over. She placed her hand gently on his nose and without a word acknowledged his status and their partnership in the world.

The Living Ranch

"The Farmers are the founders of Civilization." - Daniel Webster

Peg now had a new life but something she was certainly comfortable with. After the passing of Buck, she rearranged and rebuilt much of his home on the farm. She grew plants everywhere, inside and out. She also found a way to make a pond and populate it with local plants and animals. With all of Buck's animals and the addition of her own, the place became alive with noises both day and night. This made it feel comfortable to go outside and look at the stars late at night. One felt surrounded by layers of animals who were watching out for you and themselves. Any disturbance created a cacophony of sounds, rousing all of those in close proximity.

A long time ago, she had changed her name to Persephone, Goddess of Spring. Most people still called her Peg however they felt that the new name was apropos. For years after the passing of Buck, people gathered on her farm around Springtime. They looked for the new shoots of vegetation and remembered the myth of Persephone; the one where she was thought to be pushing up the plants and flowers in an attempt to escape Hades. Pluto had abducted her and took her to the underworld where she tried to leave every year. The new name stuck as the people of the new village recognized Peg's (Persephone's) talent at growing flowers, plants and crops. She also became renown as a great horse person, training people to ride and conducting therapeutic sessions for those who needed it.

Her daily routine included getting up at dawn to feed the animals (she referred to them as 'critters') then tending to her farm needs including working the fields and planting her vegetable gardens. She would come into town periodically to pick up supplies but for the most part worked the farm. As a result of her labors, the town was provided fresh vegetables, flowers and the main staples of food (corn, beans and squash).

At night she painted and created jewelry which the local population purchased periodically. All in all, she made a good living, with anything extra going to the animals. They appreciated it and the farm became an idyllic place to live.

During this period, she hired a helper, a young girl named Leah. She came in initially to help keep the barn clean and take care of the horses. Soon however she became indispensable and helped Peg with any task that needed to be taken care of. Leah had a lot of innate talents especially in the creative arts. She could act extremely well and would participate in almost every play that was put on the theatre company in town. She could memorize pages of dialogue and remember intricate dance moves. The animals knew she was special and treated her in a unique way. Not the same as how they treated Peg. Every once in a while, Leah would dance in the fields and if horses were near, they would start moving around as well, expressing themselves through motion.

Peg found this helpful as well as entertaining. One day Leah was feeding the horses. When they were done eating they started to meander about looking for something to do.

"Are you going to dance with them today," asked Peg?

"Yeah, I was thinking about it, maybe something new."

"Like the twist?"

"No, probably more like the Macarena. I was wondering last night what the horses would do if they saw repeated motions and especially if it's the same music. I brought a radio with a memory chip that has the song on it."

"Great idea, go for it!"

Leah, went back to the bard to retrieve the radio and chip. Once she returned she set up the radio near the middle of a gathering of horses. She then played the music, not too loud at first. While the music played she backed up from the radio and started the dance moves. The horses, stopped what they were doing and watched her intently.

Then at some point, they started to move, some ran and some pranced but all reacted. It was quite the scene. Peg started laughing and the birds who could see the show started making noise. Soon it was pandemonium,

223

certainly which after the passing of Buck, was needed badly. Transitions are part of our lives.

Soon the music was over and everything went back to normal. A calm took over on the farm, Leah picked up her equipment and after putting them away, went back to work taking care of the animals.

Peg went back to work as well. This time she was training a young horse in the round pen. It had a surcingle around it's belly which simulated the feel of a saddle. It also had long reins on it and the process of training was called 'ground driving." The horse could feel the tugs of the teacher through its bit. This way, when a rider was on a saddle, the sensations would be the same. She would coax the horse into going clockwise for a while, then say "Whoa." If the horse stopped quickly and faced her, then Peg would walk over and praise her. If the horse did otherwise, then Peg would continue to work it until it understood the meaning of the command. The positive feedback always works best. The horse worked clockwise then counter-clockwise for several minutes. Eventually teacher and pupil had an understanding and everyone was happy. The horse realized that it works a lot less when it follows instructions.

If a horse is tended to every day for say an hour or so, a strong bond occurs between it and its master. At this point, when training is going well, the horse learns about all of the subtle hints the rider is giving it. This includes the way the rider talks, holds the reins, moves his/her feet (forward, backward, inward) and the position in the saddle. It all matters and is a complex language that allows the horse to perform extraordinary feats when there is a strong sense of trust present.

She put together trail rides for anyone who was interested. This included several gentle horses and a ride through the woods, around lakes and in open pastures. People would gather near the farm, Peg and her helpers would come out and prepare the horses with blankets and saddles. They would also place the bits in the horses's mouthes and get the reins placed around the saddle horn. The riders were be introduced to the horses and helped into their saddles. Once everyone was ready, Peg would lead them down the trails at a leisurely pace and typically Leah would bring up the rear. Leah learned to ride well and more importantly she learned to communicate with the animals. The rides were at a leisurely pace, and the participants learned to relax as the hoses led them down the trails and through the woods. It became an opportunity for reflection and most of the people who took these rides did so for relaxation and contemplation.

As Buck used to say, "horses are a reflection of your soul." They feel your emotions and when they get used to you, will react to your tiniest inputs. It can get to the point when you learn to ride well, that you think "left" and the horse knows it and responds appropriately. Buck, Peg and Leah all understood the instinct and could relax in it's knowledge.

Peg knew the language well and could convince most any horse that she was not a threat. The response was typically one of submission and trust. People used to ask her why she liked them so much and her response was always "because they are honest." Leah learned as much as possible from Peg and together they taught the next generation how to respect and appreciate the animal kingdom.

Frank goes for a Walk

"*A human being without the proper empathy or feeling is the same as an android built so as to lack it, either by design or mistake. We mean, basically, someone who does not care about the fate which his fellow living*

227

creatures fall victim to; he stands detached, a spectator, acting out by his indifference. John Donne's theorem that 'No man is an island,' but giving that theorem a twist: that which is a mental and a moral island is not a man."

- Phillip Dick

Frank on the other hand was not human, in fact far from it but not really. In fact for those who know him best he is described as "more human than human." Frank was a late generation android who's software came out of government laboratories with a combination of state of the art techniques and dubious design goals. He was beyond genius by human standards as he remembered everything he learned. In artificial intelligence there are generally two approaches, top down and bottom up. Top down describes a technique where all information available is compared to a recent experience and correlations are drawn. Bottom up architectures use a blank slate (sometimes referred to as a 'tabula rasa') where neural networks learn from experience. Frank had both architectures built in to him and as a result produced superior memory engrams.

Working with humans was a constant source of

confusion for Frank; humans do not have perfect memories, they invent facts and generally find their way to advancement by what appears to be pure luck. The truth of human advance is a lot more complicated than that however Frank only could try to understand what he sensed. Day to day interactions caused him to have to guess (using sophisticated algorithms) what he was expected to do and how he was expected to act. Fundamentally he based his actions on statistical probabilities for success. When able, he found a way to hide from the others so he could keep the "noise" out.

Humans sensed his confusion when they talked to him and got to know him. He would hesitate for a fraction of a second if he heard contradictory information or an opinion based on incomplete knowledge. Humans quickly realized that he had to make a decision as to how to proceed next when talking with them. Most of the time, the interactions were appropriate and even sometimes humorous. Fundamentally however, he was in some sort of cyber pain and the others came to be aware of it. These conversations revealed his thoughts:

"Good morning, Frank."

"Good morning to you as well, Stephen."

"How was your evening?"

"Very similar to the rest of my day, just fewer people around to talk to."

"Was that good or bad?"

..."Good, I suppose."

"Can you elaborate?"

"Yes."

"No, I'm sorry. That was a confusing question. What made your experience good last night?"

"The lack of human interaction allowed me to make more progress."

"What are you making progress towards?"

"I am formulating specific answers to important questions that dominate human thought. I need to understand why they are so important and thus why people spend so much time using their energy to pursue these questions."

"Can you give me an example?"

"They seem to be driven on several issues, notably space travel. I do not understand the logic of wanting to risk their lives to find other places to live."

"Can you access your human history files to answer that question?"

"I find many answers to that question; it appears that some humans are in a constant state of exploration.

They seem unsatisfied with the status quo and want more. It seems built into their DNA."

"That is generally true, Frank. We humans have always explored, taken risks and acted irrationally while pursuing a goal. It's our nature."

"That does not make sense, Stephen."

"I think it might help to understand that humans are curious and that taking risks can be thrilling, especially when you are successful. Sometimes we are willing to fail many times before we achieve our goal. Some of us will work decades to try and discover something important."

"That still does not make sense, Stephen."

"Well let's look at it from another angle. You are the uberman, the superman or what Frankenstein was really intended to be. This means perfection, strength and talent. You see us as having portions of those ideals. For instance, some of us are better and are more talented than others. You have no such restrictions. With all of that capability, what do you choose to do?"

"When we arrive at our destination, I will leave."

"Hmmm, where will you go?"

"Far."

"Why?"

"Because I can, because I need to."

"So you will leave us to go explore?"

"I will leave you to search."

"And what will you be searching for?"

"Peace, others like me, something new to learn."

"Those are good things to search for, except for maybe others like you. I believe you are unique. You will find an abundance of things to learn about out there. Ironically you will probably come back after your initial search to be with us again."

"Why is that?"

"Because you need us to make another like you. And I hope you will need us to tell your stories about discovery to. You must remember that you were designed in our own image, which includes our advantages and our flaws."

Frank was silent, signaling a significant amount of concentration on the words he had just heard. There was a certain logic in them and he had no choice but to give them high priority.

For the rest of the voyage, Frank did his job and took his breaks when appropriate. He never discussed his conversations with Stephen to anyone else and kept his plans to himself.

Once they arrived at the new planet, Frank made

sure he had assisted in every way and when he was given the opportunity to go down to the surface, he immediately took off into the woods. Others gave chase for a while but soon gave up as Frank could move quickly and for a very long time. Soon he was many miles away.

He did not understand that he had left behind people who valued him as a friend. These were people like Peg who valued his honesty and his ability not to judge. For many, these attributes were a relief. During his design, most of the engineers were concerned about controlling his will and making sure he did not fall into the traps of so many human frailties like egocentrism, hate and ambition. To control that attributes, they had to leave his honesty algorithms fully functional which controlled his ego, emotions and ambitions. Humans could stand to learn from this approach.

When he left, people mourned but soon they had to put their emotions aside to concentrate on their numerous tasks. Most assumed he would either return or be found by the ever increasing surveillance network that was being implemented. Frank was smart enough and agile enough to stay away from the network for a long time.

After his escape, he found a series of caves many miles distant and spent several days there. He learned quite a bit about the local flora and fauna which guided him for the rest of his journey. After his stay there he continued at a more moderate pace as far away from the village as possible until eventually he was hundreds of miles away. The land was indeed foreign with lots of unknown animals and vegetation. There came a point during his trek where he sensed that some of the animals were intelligent, some very intelligent as they would maneuver around him and formed symbols or made melodic sounds. He had no reference in his data base as to what they were trying to communicate to him. His neural networks attempted to understand but they needed more time and inputs to complete the tasks. He simply took note of the phenomenon and continued walking.

At some point, very deep in the wilderness, he came across structures that had been purposely built. He knew intelligence was required here but the structures were periodic and did not have the sense of being used for shelters. These were more like shrines or other contemplative venues. As he continued deeper into this area, he noticed that periodic structures gave way to designs that had other purposes. They looked like replications of the solar system or sophisticated maps of the stars above. In all cases the structures looked new or at least made of a material that showed no age. He would feel it and slide his hands across the building and found them extremely smooth. The 3D structures were designed in such a way that from one angle they look like a complex object and ninety degrees from that angle they look like an another complex object, they same we found to be a way create complex memories structures in computers. Algorithms now create cubes of memory space with at least three times the data.

There was another sensation while exploring these areas, one not from the fundamental senses but from his own circuits. He could tell that his timing circuits and logic circuits were not performing 100%. They needed frequent calibration and restarts. This meant that there was significant amounts of electro magnetic radiation associated with the structures. For his own safety he chose to keep moving and simply take note of the position and attributes of this area.

Even after he had left, he still had electromagnetic disturbances albeit at a lesser intensity. After a few days more, they were essentially gone. However he had residual effects long after this experience, where he could recall an image of one of the structures for instance and see flashes of sentient beings superimposed as if they were standing there looking at him. When he was there he saw nothing like this, only when he was gone for several days did these apparitions appear.

He continued on and just filed his experiences for later retrieval and analysis. He found lakes and oceans, mountain ranges and deserts. All like Earth but all different. Again every few days he would run into animals that appeared to be intelligent. In all cases the animals treated him with curiosity and never became aggressive. They watched him in a neutral manner, all in the same way. It never occurred to him to try to interact with any of them and as a result, he never had a chance to get to know them better. Many were large, like bears and deer, many were small like dogs and rabbits. None of them were identical to animals on Earth, just similar morphologically.

After two months of walking and many hundreds of miles away from people, he paused. He had thought about all of his interactions with the humans and in one particular case, had to resolve a big problem.

Now that the colony was getting established, the commander, Randy, would be making life miserable for the people. He had been a terrible manager when they were traveling through space and he had heard dozens of stories of his rages, intolerance, ego centrism and other faults. It would not be fair to the villagers to have to live their lives under his iron fist. The only logical thing to do was to retrieve him and bring him out into the wilderness so that they could live their normal lives.

Frank turned back to return the way he came. He noticed that during his walk he could hear the faint sounds of drones. He knew that eventually they would find him especially now that he was coming back. But it would take time and Frank was expert at keeping himself out of the cameras' eyes. He calculated that he had a very good chance of returning back to the village un-noticed and retrieving the commander.

As he returned, he passed through the monument area once again. And once again he started to have sensations with anything associated with electro magnetic fields. This was annoying but not dangerous; he simply kept reseting his circuits and ignoring false messages. Once he got to the heart of the buildings, he noticed something interesting. His map of the area on his initial visit implied that the building had either changed shape or moved. At one point he was passing a large flat wall and imprinted upon it was a circle of animals, mostly horses, forming a circle around a fallen person in a field. Frank had no idea what it meant or that it was a replication of the death of Buck. Frank continued on and now had the sense that the buildings were somehow alive and somehow connected with the odd behavior of the animals he had encountered. Again, he took notes for later retrieval and analysis.

He continued towards the village which by now was several days away and he continued to avoid the drones and satellite cameras. As far as the satellites were concerned, he knew the exact orbit of the mother ship and could easily calculate when the cameras on board it could see him. He would freeze all movement in the densest part of the forests or hide within caves. Most of the time he was able to elude detection, however a few technicians aboard the ship could sense that something was going on. They tried to alert the Commander about it but he seemed totally uninterested.

Frank finally made it back to the village and found a place, several miles away, that he could both hide and use as an observation platform. He knew that no one was looking for him and he could also see when they launched the observation drones so he could stay hidden. He stayed here and observed the activity in the village day and night. He witnessed the transformation of the people he once knew from crew members to villagers. It was if they had been transported back to Earth but did not know it. Frank watched people work and play and generally live a relaxed, ideal life. His observations taught him more about human psychology than he had learned while in close quarters with them on the ship. Interestingly, is observations reminded him of the book 'Frankenstein' where the superior being watched a family and tried to understand their actions.

He wondered what had happened to the commander; he never saw him in the village or (when he could make out what people were saying) heard any reference to him. He surmised that the general feeling that the Commander was just a bad experience allowed them to forget him, and forget him they did, at least for the moment.

Maybe a New Life Form?

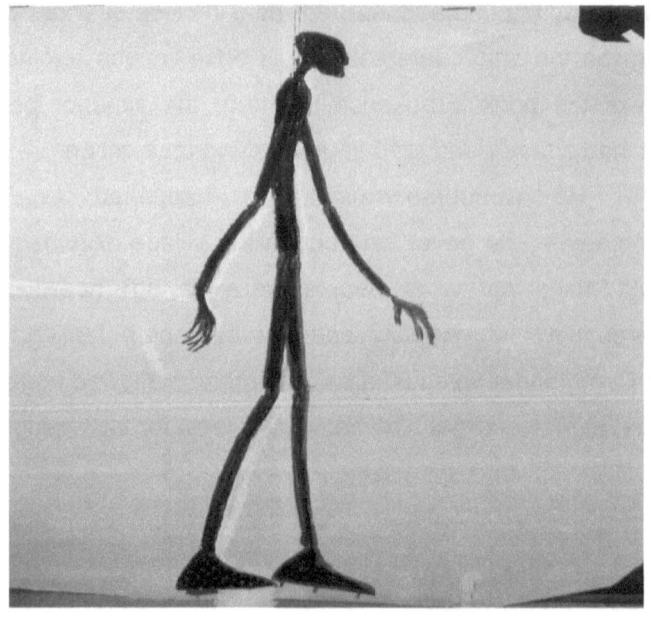

"We meet aliens every day who have something to give us. They come in the form of people with different opinions." - William Shatner

Martin had remained on the ship, unable to

transport to the ground due to his frail condition. He was not ill just weak from his lack of exercise and changed forever by this significant exposure to weightlessness. He was almost 10" longer than when he walked on board the ship. He was also 50 pounds lighter, his arms and legs were very thin. His head had swelled up a bit and his eyes tended to bulge out. He moved gracefully but slowly between the walls, floor and ceiling of his new quarters in the center of the ship. He could no longer spend more than a few minutes in real gravity as his heart had to work so hard to keep his brain nourished. The weight itself was like a normal person having a 100 pound suit on at all times. He could sit for a while but walking was a significant chore.

He chose this life, even after all of the pleas from his crew mates and orders from his bosses. He chose to move away from gravity and allow weightlessness to change him into something new.

The something new he sensed early on when he spent more than a few hours floating near the center of the ship. It was like a euphoria, his eyes glazed and his mind wandered. This effect replaced by the ability to concentrate heavily on whatever task he was performing. He sensed that this new life was a better one, one that he could sacrifice certain things to obtain. Strength was not

241

needed to move about however his mind and its capabilities seemed to be growing in astounding ways. He had thoughts about subjects which did not interest him in the past. Science, philosophy and religion all meant something much more now. He spent all of his spare time reading and absorbing these subjects. He found that his memory had improved significantly and with the help of the implants in his body, he could access information from the ship's data banks with ease.

The meaning of life was becoming clear to Martin. There were times when he floated for hours just piecing together his thoughts to form a new way of looking at the Universe. It all seemed to have a purpose. It also seemed to be a place where biological beings were destined to explore. Intelligence was the driving force behind DNA enhancements. People, he felt, were being pulled into new realms of thought and discovery. 'Towards what?" he wondered. Where were we going? And why were we going there?

Martin sensed that there was a path we needed to follow in the Universe. We were attracted by the wondrous discoveries that found as we went further and deeper into the unknown. He tried to juxtapose his thoughts with the history of religion on Earth. Animism was followed by

Polytheism, then Monotheism, then Pantheism and finally Atheism. There was a predilection among humans towards some sort of spiritual thought. Most of the time there were multiple, sometimes conflicting types of religion. Certainly many millions of people had died for religious reasons, but they continued anyway. God was defined in a million ways and those who could be objective tried to synthesize a super religion. Others decided that God was just a projection of human beings, an ideal, a way to define moral and ethical rules of behavior.

Fundamentally, Martin found something more pure, a sense of spirituality that could be only defined without words, as they would constrict an honest description. All languages together could come close but it got down to a sense, a sense of pre-ordained purpose. Martin relished in the thought as he realized that the answer was in space. Space exploration would lead to the answers many people sought. What some sages have discovered is that there is an overwhelming amount of life out there; so much that statistically we are in the middle of the intelligence range. This means that there are entities out there we will never understand but have vast knowledge of who we really are.

His voyage had really only begun as once the technical details of radiation and self-sustainment were dealt with, his life would be inordinately long.

At one point, Martin distinctly heard voices of people praying. I was at a certain place during the voyage and the effect lasted for several hours. He interpreted them as voices sent into the Universe meant for the Gods. He had no idea where they were going or even if they were real. His senses told him what he was perceiving was true but any technical means of verifying could not be found. He tried to be objective and scientific about it, took notes and tried various types of equipment to see if there was any physical phenomena going on. He continued hunting until the effect dissipated and was never felt again. This added to his wonderment and verified that his spiritual predilections were not born from nothingness.

He had visions too, they started around the time they went into orbit around the new planet. They were mostly snippets of images not understood, however he experienced a vivid one right around the time of Buck's death. He had clear images of horses in a circle around a body. There were other circles as well, mostly of different animals. Martin wondered why predator and prey animals would form these shapes next to each other. The visions lasted for a few days, the body disappeared and was replaced by a mound. Martin dreamt one night about the circles and that they were sending circularly polarized signals into space. The mound in his dream hosted a tree that grew to a hundred meters with branches just five meters from the ground. It was a profound dream, Martin woke up with the visions still flashing in his mind. He started to have the feeling that this world was a special world, that he could sense it's greatness and that the humans on or near it were going to be surprised by the amazing attributes it would slowly reveal.

He had further visions and dreams about the structures on the planet, although no one except Frank had actually seen them. One important idea he learned from these apparitions was that some civilization had or now does the reverse of what humans had done. The civilization relishes life and encourages its growth. Humans had a legacy of overrunning animal habitats and forcing many species into extinction. They had plundered and destroyed billions of life forms in an effort to sustain themselves and assert their dominance.

By the time the others had redefined Martin as a priest, he was starting to write down his thoughts in a missal that he thought would be more meaningful in the years to come. He dedicated his life to recording his thoughts and trying to make sense of the feeling and vibes around him.

People took him somewhat seriously but in the end learned to leave him alone in the ship and continue with the many tasks they were responsible for. In other words, they moved on.

The Scribe's Job

"This then is the Scribe's direct purpose: The making of useful things legibly beautiful." - Edward Johnston

As the scribe and chronicler of the voyage and village life, Stephen had to take notes in a journal every day. His observations became the basis of the beginning of the new civilization and would be read for a thousand years thereafter.

He described the voyage that has been adapted to the narrative in the previous pages. After the landing and developing of the community, he interviewed all of the crew members. Most made private observations, to be revealed at a later time. Many made public ones. The vast majority of the public ones described the overbearing command style and the relief they experienced once on the new world. Once the process of transferring people to the ground commenced and was deemed safe the commander disappeared into his cabin and ordered all meals in. He sometimes responded to electronic messages but he seemed completely annoyed that anyone would try to contact him. Soon, the communications diminshed to zero. His staff took up the slack and made all the important decisions from that point on. Not surprisingly, few people worried about him and his sequester. All had been derided and humiliated by him during the voyage so he had few friends. He was quickly and readily forgotten. For the weeks and months he stayed behind doors, he planned his escape Stephen found out. Although Stephen had tried on numerous occasions to interview the commander, he always refused. Indirectly, Stephen found out that the commander was ordering provisions and camping equipment to be placed inside his private shuttle. He had chosen his items carefully and the indications were that he was planning a long "camping" trip.

Once the shuttle was completely full, the Commander asked Stephen to come to his quarters for an interview.

Stephen went immediately, the hallway to the commander's cabin was abandoned; everyone in his chain of command had gone to the surface to start their new lives. By the looks of the debris and open doors, they all went quickly.

Stephen made it to the commanders quarter and knocked on the door.

"Come in."

He entered and found the quarters in perfect shape, in fact pristine. Looking around, he found it Spartan as well with no evidence that anyone was really living there.

The commander spoke first:

"Sit down there, I want this to be a private discussion and not to be published for one year. Is that clear?"

"Yes sir, I understand your need for priva......."

"You will indeed, if I find out you violated my orders I will hunt you down."

"Understood."

"Now, here is what I want to talk about. I am leaving this ship and everyone associated with it. I will be going to the far reaches of this world and intend to live out my life by myself."

"Ok."

"The reason I am doing this is manyfold. I do not like this crew and have found them incompetent, lacking of any military order and frankly an embarrassment to be associated with. I have never met so many dumb smart people in my life and its been extremely difficult to manage them."

"Understood."

"There are other reasons besides my contempt for these clowns. In the weeks before we landed I learned that this place contains some extraordinary intelligence. They visited me in my quarters well before we entered orbit. I told no one because they would not understand. I learned that there are buildings and monuments down there that are extremely important. They are all over the planet and I have chosen a site to land at which I will never reveal to anyone. I do not ever want to be contacted or searched for in any way. You may tell your people this and I am sure they will comply. All right that's it, I am leaving. Stay in this room for the next several hours, do not contact anyone or set off any alarms, if you do so, I will remotely command this ship to enter the atmosphere. Do you understand?"

"Clearly, sir."

With that curt exchange, the commander got up, gave Stephen a hard look, and left. The door shut smartly and Stephen just looked at it for a long while, contemplating the gruff nature of the conversation which was more like a lecture.

"Good riddance, he thought."

He stayed for the prescribed hours, going through the cabin looking for any clue as to how this horrible person came to be. The remaining clothes were immaculately placed in drawers and closets. There were no personal effects and the computers had been completely disabled.

After the wait, he left the cabin, turned and shut the door to both the quarters and the bad memories and walked back to his cabin. Once there he had messages waiting for him. The commander was observed for the last time walking the halls, talking to no one, entering his shuttle and commanding the depressurization of the shuttle bay. The remaining crew members observed the shuttle leaving the vicinity of the mother ship then it went stealth. Few knew that this shuttle had special paint on it and special electronics to completely confuse the radar operators. All that was left was a trace of heat, soon it was gone as the shuttle disappeared from all monitors.

The crew felt a combination of interest as well as relief. The commander was gone and he obviously did not want anyone to know where he went. That was fine with them and the monitors were quickly placed back into their "normal" modes.

Stephan sat back in his chair, watching the vanishing act unfold. Soon the messages stopped showing up on his screen as no one really cared anymore.

He wondered why the commander had not revealed his information about the buildings and visits they had experienced when they were close. He assumed the technicians who had given the information to him were under strict orders not to reveal the information to others. So now Stephen was the holder of the important information and would be in a real quandary if their safety was challenged by these new entities. Stephen would have to sit on it for now.

At the same time he was thinking about this, the commander was finalizing his approach to his new home. Somehow he knew that a particular clearing in an area almost exactly opposite the village was where he needed to land. He placed his shuttle on autopilot and auto land, it slowed down and arced toward the clearing then gently touched down. He opened the door and deployed the air stair. "Nobody here," he thought as he walked down and felt the ground of a new planet. He explored the immediate area a bit then returned to the shuttle to completely shut down it's systems and put every system in hibernation mode. Solar cells on the top of the shuttle would keep the craft alive for ever at this low level of activity. He covered the ship with camouflage netting that let just enough sunlight in for the solar panels.

The commander, or actually not the commander now; Randy proceeded to pull gear and essential supplies out of the shuttle for the next several hours and set up camp. As night grew close he had a shelter, food and a bottle of whiskey to enjoy. Late that evening his final thought before he passed out was "I hated all of those people."

Stephen on the other hand felt a relief just like the rest, that a very negative, long lasting experience was at an end.   He knew that no one would go looking for the commander.

He continued his interviews and focused his attention on the runaway android, Frank. Everyone knew the basic story but Stephen wondered why he had acted so strangely. Now, some technicians were murmuring about sensor detections of apparitions and false images. They felt something was down there, near the village, but they did not know why. There were smears and false echoes on their monitors and the imaginative among them considered them the motions of someone or something that did not want to be found. A particularly bright technician wrote a program that listed the false echoes chronologically and found that they followed a line from the wilderness to the village. The same technician found that coincidentally after the departure of the commander from the main ship, the apparition was on the move again, as if it had known the commander was moving. It was observed moving away from the village at a high rate of speed, the technicians knew the capabilities of the android and also knew that it could be on the move day and night. They correlated the appearance of the ghostly radar and visible images with the speed per hour compensating for terrain. The correlations were high that Frank was indeed the object of interest in their monitors.

Frank was observed moving in a generally western direction for several weeks. Somewhere toward the exact opposite side of the planet from the village. The image moved consistently day and night until it reached it's goal which was indeed the opposite side of the planet. The image remained there, in a very particular place, for another week.

Meanwhile, the technicians moved their telescopes and sensors to the new, remote area and started taking data.

It wasn't long until they knew that Frank had found the commander. It was not obvious how, considering the commander told no one where he was going and somehow Frank, who was in hiding, suddenly understood where the commander had landed.

Stephen took note of all of these developments and wondered, as they all did, what would happen next.

But he also had to complete his interviews with everyone else both on the ship and on the ground. He chose to finish the ship first then transition himself and his life to the village. He would remain there unless called back.

Next he wanted to talk to Martin again, who was

certainly floating about in zero g near the center of the ship. Stephen had to move to one of the spokes holding the outer ring, then up the spoke through lesser and lesser gradients of gravity to the center where all things floated. Although Martin was expecting him, he was not easy to find. Stephen had a series of cryptic of addresses based on rib numbers and storage areas. Eventually, he did find Martin and it took him a while to get over the image.

Martin was long, thin, pale with an enlarged head and eyes. Stephen thought instantly of the ideas Earth people had about extraterrestrials coming out of flying saucers. No one spoke for a minute or two to allow Stephen to get over the shock.

"Martin?"

"Yes, hello Stephen."

"How are you?"

"Doing very well, thank you."

"So, no ill effects from the constant weightlessness?"

"No, not really. It's been a long road but now I feel amazing, especially mentally. There is significantly more oxygen in my brain as my bodily functions seem to be aimed at nourishing it."

"That's good, as long as you're physically okay. I

mean, you have changed morphologically quite a bit. As long as you feel okay. By the way, what do the doctors say about these changes?"

"It's interesting, they are a bit mystified about how the changes have not caused any major problems with my organs and skeletal system. They were concerned that all of the stretching and pressure changes would stress out my body but it seems to be adapting quickly. The downside of course is that I can no longer stand in 1 g. I have spoken to some engineers who think I can use an exoskeleton to allow me to visit the surface for instance but they are still concerned about how my cardio vascular system will react. We are still talking about it. But again, the doctors see nothing wrong and as you can expect, want to study me."

"Ok, good. Now for the mental part, can you describe how you are doing cognitively?"

"Of course. On Earth I used to run and exercise quite a bit. My mind worked at it's peak when I did this and I used to miss this feeling when I did not exercise. Now however that good feeling has returned but at a much higher level. In fact I can concentrate on something for hours; I find myself staring out a window and thinking about cosmology and hours later shaking myself awake. My brain is near perfection, I can only guess at how much more someone like Einstein or Newton could have accomplished in the same state. It's hard to explain but I am now getting to the point where I am wasting time doing anything else but thinking."

"Understood. And good for you I think. We could always use the extra insight into existence. Where to you think our civilization is headed?"

"Good question and the short answer is you will be okay. The best thing we have done for ourselves is get away from Earth. The best thing for Earth is that we leave it; humans destroy most of what they take for granted. Clean air and water were assumed to be everywhere but greed and self aggrandizement almost killed everything on the planet. The number of species and the quality of the environment has plummeted since the industrial revolution and we have produced toxic waste that will eat away at the Earth for thousands of years to come. As you know we are but one group of colonists that got away. We need to learn from the past by the way, or we are doomed to repeat it. Technology has been a great help but we need to always keep on long terms goals in sight. The other colonists know these things and I hope that more will leave our planet. If you look around our new place (and I hope to do this soon) you will find it stunningly wonderful. The air is pure, the flora and fauna are amazing. Well, this is how Earth used to be, now they find the animals in the zoos and the plants in the greenhouses."

"Yes, Martin, unfortunately you are right, we shredded that planet."

"A shame but an opportunity to learn about ourselves. Humans are incredibly intelligent, but as you will find out we are as primitive as ants compared to what is waiting out there for us. We have not yet begun to ask the right questions. Remember what Carl Sagan said, 'The Stars call for us' and he was right. The only answers to our burning questions are out there waiting for us. All of the groups who have left Earth need to find a good place to live then continue to propagate out to the stars to give humans any chance of long term success. If we had stayed on Earth, we would have been doomed; and as you can see on the daily reports coming from there, life is hell. We were very lucky to escape, Stephen."

"Yes, we all feel that Martin. On another subject, what future to you have?"

"Mine will be long and prosperous. It will also be dependent on the quality of technology. Without it I am doomed, with it I know I will live at least 400 years."

"How do you know that?"

"The doctors have discovered that my cells are replicating (that is with this new body) perfectly. On Earth, hydra, jelly fish and lobsters all are immortal, they die by other means, like being eaten or accidents. The telemires in my DNA are working perfectly. They say they are not sure how long I will last but it should be at least 400 years."

"Wow, good for you, but as you say, you will need technology to allow you to live in space, that means you need this spaceship, at least for now. How are you going to maintain it once we are all gone?"

"Good question, especially considering my state. I can't go anywhere now with a large amount of gravity. Fixing problems will no doubt require that. I am going to replicate Frank, maybe several times. That will be a start. Then I will stop all artificial gravity produced by this ship."

"Yes I agree. It's interesting how we have become dependent on the robots and androids now and certainly dependent on computers."

"It's only the beginning. Now that we have passed the singularity, the robots and androids realize humans gave them life, they are thankful for that and will take care of us in the future. The super androids, ones that are magnitudes more intelligent than us will be leaving to follow our dreams."

"Interesting observation, what makes you think they will follow *our* dreams?"

"Because we designed them and they have no other point of reference. Remember, we were the people who defined logic; and logic has some very simple concepts, and, or, exclusive or, etc., so the robots and androids are unable to break out of the thinking methods we gave them. They can be faster with perfect memory, but they cannot dream, or guess or write poetry. So they use the only point of reference they have, our history; and our history is largely about exploration, conquest and determination. I mean that we look for medical cures, other planets or play football with these same ideals. Our DNA imprints on their DNA."

"Understood. It seems like you might be implying a few things. For instance, no more biologicals, too limited?"

"Yes."

"And for the advanced machines, venues in space for safety."

"Yes."

"And they would find the raw materials to maintain their existence on un-inhabited asteroids, moons and planets?"

"Yes."

"So what are the chances that these entities have already been created and are out there now?"

"Significant. As you know, we have found out that biology really can come from primordial environments with readily available chemistry. So if we assume understood biologies are out there, we can assume biological needs and wants and therefore biological logic."

"That's lots of assumptions."

"True, but this is a big Universe. And you know about the findings of the planet hunters many years ago, they found biology everywhere."

"That's true."

"And you know that we have had encounters with superior intelligence."

"Like what they are now talking about on the planet's surface?"

"Yes, the technicians have lit up our Internet with strange readings. There is something else going on with Frank as well. He disappeared then they think he came back to watch us from distance, then when the commander left, it seems Frank understood this and disappeared again in the direction of the commander's landing sight. He has also passed by an area of buildings and unusual energy emanations."

"Wow, I did not know that."

"Yes, I think we have a lot more to learn about this place."

Stephen sat back for a moment to consider all of the words he just heard. Martin senses his need to think and said:

"I need to go back to work, please visit anytime."

Martin reached out one of his very long arms and pushed strategically on the wall to propel himself perfectly down the circular hallway and back to his dwelling. He did not expect a reply and was quickly gone from sight.

Stephen watched him glide away effortlessly. He was full of thought from the interview and had to write the details down to keep everything in order. He decided to retrace his steps back to his cabin, have a glass of wine and write down notes about his encounter with an advanced human species.

His writings and wine drinking took longer than expected and after dinner and more wine, Stephen decided to call it a day. He opened his window shade, turned off all of the lights and for the first time saw the faint ring of ice particles the astronomers were talking about. Camomile had discovered them while they were inbound but the details were deep in the data and were not resolved until

Kevin O. Shoemaker

just recently.

"I will talk to Camomile tomorrow," he thought. Right before he went to bed he sent her an email to make sure she was available. He then crawled into bed and thought about his conversations and how to put them into perspective. "This is a new world." were his last coherent thoughts before he fell asleep.

The next morning, he arose with his head full of images, especially of Martin floating in space, looking just like the aliens people on Earth thought would be coming for us. This he found totally interesting, that humans would morph into our alien dreams from so long ago by living too long in weightlessness.

He had his tea and breakfast, then reviewed his email responses from the day before. Camomile had indeed responded and told him to stop by in the afternoon. That meant that Stephen had to make sure he had a seat on the afternoon shuttle. He texted the flight department to get his reservation and received a confirmation code.

As he was going to be on the ground for a long while, he gathered his important belongings including clothes, packed and made sure his cabin was tidied up.

After about an hour, he took his bags, headed out the shuttle hangar and secured his belongings on board.

As he was waiting for take off, he noticed Rudy walking around the shuttle doing a pre-flight.

"You flying this today?"

"Yep, it's my turn."

"Any issues?"

"None, the shuttle looks good and the weather looks good. We should be able to depart on time. Going to get some ground time?"

"Yeah, I need to interview Camomile today and see how the adjustment to the new planet is going."

"Camomile? Great, tell her hello for me."

"I shall. Rumor has it that you two are getting along."

"Can't keep a secret very long around here. Yes we are seeing each other quite a bit. For now however I need to finish my pre-flight. Why don't you sit in the cockpit with me, right seat?"

"Okay, great. I will board now, sorry about the interruption."

"No problem. I just need to concentrate."

"Understood, see you on board."

Stephen turned and climbed the air stair to go inside. While everyone else turned right to go and sit down in the main cabin, he got to turn left and go into the cockpit.

As he got closer, a flight attendant stood in his way.

"Sorry, you have to sit in the main cabin."

"I just talked to Rudy and he asked me to sit right seat in the cockpit so we could talk during the flight."

"Okay, standby for a second, and let me check."

"He tapped on his wrist phone and sent a text message to Rudy. Within seconds the reply came back."

"Okay, you are good to go. Please follow me."

The attendant walked Stephen to the cockpit door, opened it and motioned him in.

"Careful with the switches and buttons."

"I will be, I have actually been in a few cockpits over the years."

"Good. Make yourself comfortable and push that button (motioning) if you need anything."

"Thank you"

Stephen maneuvered his way to the seat, sat down and attached his seat belts. Actually it was more like a harness, with two shoulder straps , a lap strap and one between the legs. He surveyed the flight deck, showing the shuttle status, flight plan and any warnings. It looked sophisticated yet simple. Multiple computers sampled sensors thousands of times per second and displayed messages when necessary. The flight controls were simple, two hand grips, one left and one right, and one set of rudders. There were head's up displays on both the pilot and co-pilot positions showing holographic presentations of the present position, future flight path and critical flight data. The lighting was subdued so his eyes were starting to get dark adapted with Rudy opened the door and entered.

"Comfy?"

"Very, thank you for letting me fly in the cockpit. I used to fly at home quite a bit as a flight instructor and commercial pilot."

"Yeah, I heard. I had to clear you for this seat and they told me about all of the certificates you have. So if I black out you can take over."

"Maybe, where's the parachute?"

"Very funny. it's way in the back. I suggest you run out here screaming through the passenger cabin to make sure you get there first and let the others know we're doomed."

"You got it Captain."

"Ok, time to get serious."

"Understood, let me know if I can assist."

"Okay."

Rudy then started the process of configuring the shuttle for take off. As he threw switches and set dials, the warning signs on the multi function displays started to disappear. He pushed system test buttons that sometimes engaged alarms and/or blinking lights. He read from a check list keeping his thumb on the item of interest as he worked down. At some point all of the warnings were gone, he finished his list and it was time to fly. He got on the radio.

"Traffic control, this is Thales shuttle number 3 ready for departure."

"Shuttle 3 traffic control, stand by for depressurization."

"Roger, shuttle 3 standing by."

Flashing yellow lights in the launch bay started to flash, alarms sounded and soon, a hissing sound could be heard. Rudy watched his displays for outside air pressure as well as indicators for inside air pressure, just to make sure there were no leaks in the hull of the shuttle.

"Pressure check good, control."

"Roger that, cycle will now continue."

The hissing continued for a another minute or two then the sound dissipated into nothingness. Rudy rechecked his gauges and when satisfied, contacted control.

"Control, shuttle 3 has good pressure. All systems

nominal."

"Shuttle 3, control. Stand by for bay door opening."

"Shuttle 3 standing by."

In front of the shuttle stood a large door. It started to move up releasing a small amount of dust at the base as it started. Within thirty seconds it was completely open and both Rudy and Stephen with dark adapted eyes by now, could see stars.

Rudy engaged the thruster system, gripped one of the hand controllers and gently pulling back on it, levitated the shuttle about a meter above the shuttle bay floor. Again he scanned his displays and then with his other hand on the second hand controller, pushed a bit to start the shuttle moving towards the open hatch.

The shuttle moved effortlessly toward the opening, then out into space. Stars filled all of the windows with the exception of the lower few, which had the image of the planet below. They were weightless now as they left the spinning 1 g section of the space ship into the vacuum of space. Now Stephen appreciated the 5 point harness he was strapped into.

They glided for several minutes, allowing them to distance themselves from the mother ship. Soon after, Rudy reached down and engaged the flight computer, the sound of engines now increased and they felt physically pushed back into their seats. The sensation lasted for a few minutes as the attitude of the ship rolled and pitched towards a point on the horizon of the planet. Once pointed correctly, the attitude stabilized and soon the sound of rockets diminished to nothing. Silence took over as Rudy and Stephen knew from the monitors that they were moving very quickly however there was nothing but peace going on around them. This would last for another twenty minutes then the approach would commence. For now however, they quietly smiled at the blissful experience.

Stephen thought deeply about the experience. Rudy was quietly watching screens and lost in his own world which left Stephen with the opportunity to wonder why this experience was so pleasant. He thought, "people dream about flying and floating in space, they have done this for thousands of years. Does it remind them of floating in the womb? Doesn't every child as some point in their lives stretch out their arms and pretend to fly like birds? And here I am floating in my seat looking at the most beautiful sight I have ever seen through the cabin windows. What makes this so attractive? To me and to us as a civilization?"

"Having fun?"

Rudy broke the silence and train of thought coursing through Stephen's brain.

"This is absolutely amazing."

"Yes it is. I used to think flying back home was wondrous but when you do it in space, there is a much higher level of satisfaction. Oh, and a lot less turbulence." Rudy smiled at the last thought.

"You get to do this every day?"

"Most, I am building up the aviation infrastructure on the planet, that takes a lot of work and I cannot fly as much as I would like. However, when I need a break I just tell people that 'I need to get some air' and take off in my plane or sign up for a shuttle trip."

"Do most people understand this sensation?"

"No, most do not. They seem to want to get it over with. Kids seem to enjoy it and pilots who are sitting back in the passenger cabin would rather be up here."

"Hmmm, interesting. In a way it makes sense. I am amazed that most of the adults are bored with it."

"That's because they are cargo, do not understand the intricacies of flight and have other things in their minds."

"Understood. Well okay, that's the way it is then; nothing we can do about it."

"Yep, except enjoy it."

"Yes indeed."

With that said, Rudy needed to go back to work. He looked up at his head's up display and acknowledged a flashing message on the multi function display.

Rudy picked up the microphone, pushed the intercom button and said:

"Folks, this is the Captain speaking. We will be initiating our approach in a few minutes. This means that we will be slowing down, then going through some buffeting before we get to normal atmospheric flight speeds. You might notice some bright colors outside of your windows. This is completely normal, just ionized gases flowing past us. Please make sure your seat belts are fastened securely. We will be on the ground in approximately 20 minutes. Thank you."

Rudy looked at Stephen, smiled and said:

"Okay, here we go."

He pushed another button on the center console and acknowledged several messages on his display. The shuttle started to brake which pulled everyone out of their seats slightly. This went on for several minutes while the attitude of the ship changed a bit to a more nose down pitch.

Soon there was a sensation of slight turbulence,

then the ionized gases started to appear outside of the windows. Tiny sparks dances around the skin fasteners and any protruding parts of the shuttle. St. Elmo's fire mixed with fuselage heating. The buffeting went on for several minutes followed by the raising of the nose. Stephen saw clouds outside now and could sense that the shuttle had slowed down significantly. They had kept their forward velocity down to minimize heating and used their maneuvering rockets to maintain a minimal descent rate. The whole process took longer than burning through the atmosphere like the Space Shuttle so many years ago had to do. This was a lot more gentle and smoother.

Soon they were feeling the gentle bumps of atmospheric movement and gliding towards their intended landing spot. The view outside was beautiful, with forests, lakes and rivers; the same but completely different from Earth. Stephen smiled at the sight and looked forward to spending good time on the surface.

Rudy deftly maneuvered this ship down to a final approach course and after lining up to the touch down point, slowed the ship down considerably. By the time the speed had diminished to zero they were a few feet from the ground and picking up dust. With a few movements of the controls and switches, he lowered the landing gear and gently

273

settled the shuttle on the new world. The people in the cabin who had taken this trip before unbuckled, stood up and gathered their belongings.

Stephen however stayed in his seat while Rudy followed his shut down check list. Soon all was silent and Rudy reached up to a switch and actuated the door opening and air stair deployment. Noises were heard in the back of the shuttle and Rudy started to unbuckle, Stephen followed suit. Soon they smelled fresh air which after an extended stay in a space ship, was wonderful.

They both rose, gathered their things and walked towards the open fuselage door at the rear of the shuttle. The sun was bright and the air fresh. Most of the people who were in the passenger cabin had left and on their way to their particular destinations.

Once on the ground, Stephen turned to Rudy and said:

"Thanks for the great trip, Rudy. I envy your job."

"You're welcome, Stephen. Anytime you want to take the trip let me know and you can have the best seat in the office."

Rudy smiled, turned and walked back to the shuttle to do a post flight, secure the cabin and close the door.

Stephen directed his attention to the village, which

was about a quarter of a mile away. He intended to talk to several of the inhabitants and with his previous interviews, compose an overview of the transition to the new world.

On his way down the path to the central part of the village, he took note of the new smells, sounds and sights. This was indeed an idyllic place with new types of vegetation and animals. The animals in particular were unique, most were small and similar to squirrels or small deer. Off in the distance, he saw Buck's farm, now basically Peg's farm. As he walked he felt something strange as he looked at the animals. He stopped on the path and tried to find out what was different about the animals here. The ones on the farm looked familiar enough but even they were somehow different. He noticed that they all watched him with the normal curiosity, but there was something unique. It took him a while but he realized that they were all in synchrony. Their tails swished at the same times, they moved at the same time, somehow they were communicating with each other. It was a very strange sight indeed.

Stephen watched this phenomena for some time, mesmerized by its implications. At some point he or someone else would have to understand what was going on. It felt safe but it would be prudent to truly understand this new energy. He made a mental note to talk to Peg and the others at the farm to see what they thought. For now he had to continue his walk and find something to eat at the village.

Fifteen minutes later he was at the center of the village and watching people going about their business. They all looked content and appeared to be living their normal lives.

Looking around some more he found a place to eat. He went over and sat at one of the tables outside so he could continue viewing the people in their new world. Someone came over to him.

"Can I get you something to drink?"

"Please, water would be fine."

"Water it is, the special is a Rueben today?"

"Sounds good, where do you get your meat?"

"From the synthesizer, we will never kill any animals on this planet."

"Good to hear. Okay, I'll have one."

The waitress went back inside to get his order started and get his water. He sat there and watched with fascination how the people he could see were living their normal lives, just as they had on Earth, yet they were billions of miles away.

The waitress returned with his water.

"Here you go, sir."

"Thank you, oh and I have a question."

"Yes?"

"Do you like it here?"

"On this planet or at this restaurant? Well the answer to both would be yes. Is that what you meant?"

"Well I meant in general, do you like living here. It is a comfortable place? Do you have any concerns?"

"This place is wonderful. I am stress free for the first time in my life and I believe everyone else is as well. It's been a while since we had good water, air and food. I don't have any concerns. In fact far from it since the commander disappeared, that was a relief because I had to work with him every once in a while during our journey. He was beyond rude and to be honest with you, I don't care if I ever see him again."

"Well I have heard that impression about the commander from everyone. We are not sure where he went except that it seems that he chose the exact opposite of the planet from us. I doubt that anyone will go searching for him."

"I hope not. But in general this is a great place. People are settling down and living their lives like they want to."

"Good to hear, thanks for your comments."

"Are you Stephen, the scribe?"

"Yes."

"I've heard of you."

She smiled at him a special smile then turned to go back inside for his sandwich.

"Well, that was nice," he thought

She returned shortly and placed his plate and sandwich in front of him making sure it was oriented properly.

"Here you go, Stephen. Enjoy and let me know if you have any further questions."

"I shall, and thank you.....uh?"

"Leah."

"Well, thank you Leah. I will think up some more questions."

"Okay."

And with that, she was gone. He sat there eating his sandwich and viewing the people around him. It a nice sunny Spring day and everyone seemed in a good mood. This reminded him of what people so long ago on Earth wanted. They called them utopias. They were hard to come by and hard to keep. Outside influences always broke up the euphoria it seemed.

In any event, he had a few more people to talk to before he wrote his report, the one that would be sent back to Earth for review.

He finished his lunch, brought in his plates and made sure he said goodbye to Leah before he left. She seemed like a very nice person to get to know and when he was free, he would find a way to wander over and say hello.

Leaving the food area he turned left to go towards the farms and ranches. The animal activity he had witnessed still was bouncing around in his mind. Did he really see some sort of synchronization? "Probably not," he thought out loud. "I'm sure it was just a coincidence."

The walk was pleasant and he smiled as he listened to the wild life and smelled the fresh air. He knew he was really going to like life on this planet. Far from his thoughts were the odd behaviors of the Commander and the android. These mysteries would be solved someday, "just not today," he mused.

Soon he was walking toward the entrance of the ranch that Buck built. Off in the distance, he saw the mound he was buried in complete with a Maple tree like sapling in the center. He had heard the story but wanted to make sure he got the details from the current proprietor,

Peg.

As he walked toward the farmhouse, the nearby animals, mostly horses, noticed him. Their ears were up and their eyes were focused on him as he walked down the path towards the door. They followed him for a while and then as if someone soothed them, dropped their concentration and went back to grazing. All was safe in their minds. Stephen continued towards the door but before he got within twenty feet of it, Peg came around the corner of the house and greeted him.

"Hello Stephen. How are you?"

"Doing well, Peg. How are you doing?"

"Great."

"How did you know I was here?"

"Oh, the animals told me some time ago, about when you were walking down the fence line."

"That's amazing. So..how do they talk to you?"

"All of the animals here will have a change in behavior as a stranger is getting near. If they were making noise, they stop. If they were not making noise, they start. Also, once you have their attention, they are all watching you trying to determine if you are a threat. Most of the animals here are prey animals and therefore very sensitive to anything unusual. I could sense their concern and knew someone was getting closer. I could also sense that you were no threat, as they had already made that determination and went back to what they had been doing."

"Amazing, intuitive and amazing."

"No, it's just something you learn when you live on a farm. Everybody including animals, is looking out for everybody. Its a very safe place to be, they are vigilant at all hours of the day or night. In fact at night, they tend to cluster together near the farm house and if any disturbance happens, we all know about it."

Stephen smiled at the idea of this pack of diverse animals, including humans that stick together for safety. Then he said,

"It's very peaceful here."

"Yes it is, there is something about living with animals that keeps your blood pressure down. They don't care about quotas or sales figures or profit margins. They are just living their lives out."

"Indeed."

"So how can I help you?"

"Well as you know, Peg, I am chronicling how we are all doing as we adjust to this new world. I have to write a report to send back to Earth, letting them know what challenges and hardships we faced once we arrived.

Whether of not it is difficult to live off of the land, find water etc."

"Well as you can see, life here is pretty normal. The animals are happy and the people seem happy, especially since the Commander did not come with us."

"That a standard comment I am getting from the others, about the Commander."

"Where is he?"

"Well, they think he landed on the other side of the planet and that the android, Frank actually came back towards this village until the Commander landed, then left towards his general direction."

"I think there is a connection between all of these events."

"How so?"

"I can only guess why the Commander did what he did. However is some senses he must have known about our general animosity towards him and that we would not have enjoy his presence and certainly his behavior here. I am guessing that he felt that he had accomplished his goals by safely transporting us through space and now that his goal has been met, he would simply like to retire, just not with us."

"And the connection between that act and the

android?"

"It' hard to articulate this properly. But I and the animals here sense and are starting to be influenced by a greater force here. The animals above all things, are honest, and if you watch them carefully you will notice that they tend to react in a pure way to the environment around us. For instance, then Buck passed away, they were all brought together in mourning and starting doing something I had never witnessed in all my years living with animals. They formed geometric shapes around Buck's final resting place. The let me know that they wanted his body to stay were it fell and that new life would come out of the sad event."

"Wow, and how did you get all of this communicated to you?"

"Like I said, it's hard to articulate but I can tell you the experience was real. I walked among the horses for instance, where I am most comfortable, and watched them behave in a connected way. Connected between themselves and the event of his passing. They would lead me to his grave and form shapes by positioning themselves around the burial mound. They would all look at me until I accepted what they were doing. Once they senses that I understood, they went back to their normal behaviors. It was astounding to have such a clear message projected to me from these horses. The other animals were all changed during this time as well."

"What message did they project to you?"

"What I generally felt from them was that we were all safe and welcome here. I also felt that there was a significant intelligence that lives or exists here. It might be my imagination but I sometimes feel that even the plants are part of this intelligence. Sometimes they do things in synchrony that I have never witnessed. Most of the time I write if off as just a nuance of this new planet. There is so much we do not know about it. As the scientist and engineers take data the rest of us have more intuitive thoughts and general feelings. These thoughts and feelings are real and, getting back to your question, I think even the android was influenced by them. He took off into the woods as you know and stayed there. I wonder what he found?"

"Not sure, but he was observed walking through a building complex. In fact he went through the same area twice. It should probably be explored further. The idea that we are the most intelligent entities in the Universe is very self centered. We have a lot to learn and I would not be shocked to find that the source of the odd behavior is somehow connected to those buildings. We assumed they were ancient dwellings but they also might be extremely advanced."

"Probably, in any event whoever explores there should take an animal, like a horse, with them. They would probably learn more about what is really going on by observing the actions of the animal."

"Good idea, I will put that in my posts."

"When they do decide to explore the buildings, have them come here first and I will give you one of my more sensitive horses."

"Okay, I'm sure they will appreciate it."

"For now, though, I think I will return to the village and chase a waitress."

"Good hunting, Stephen. Thanks for the visit."

"Of course, I am sure I will be seeing you around. Thanks."

And with that he was off to back track his steps down the path past the animals grazing and onto the main path back to the village. As he walked he again noticed the synchrony in the animals, or so he imagined. Although not a religious person, he certainly felt a force here. It didn't feel malevolent just potentially powerful. It was as if the force considered the people just another form of animal, more intelligent than the rest perhaps but still of the same basic genetic makeup.

As he walked he also felt the paradise nature of the planet. There was harmony and beauty everywhere. The villagers had learned to respect and protect their environment and were being careful to keep all of their inputs and outputs in a contained cycle. Nothing was wasted and pollution at all costs was avoided. Actually it was not as hard as one would expect. Solar panels provided electrical power, water was recycled and wastes were processed. Their environmental foot print was no more than any other animal species.

He was getting closer now and could see the edge of the city easily. He felt drawn towards going back to the food center where the girl worked but he did not feel that acutely hungry. For now he would walk about and perchance find someone to interview again. As he walked he started to outline his final report to Earth. It would be a challenge to describe the non Earth-like qualities to those at home. He knew he had to be careful in the presentation, keep to the facts and not get too descriptive about the intuitions and general amorphous feelings he and the inhabitants were feeling on the planet.

For now, more data was needed. He decided to stop by the laboratory complex to see if Camomile the astronomer was available to talk. She would have cogent observations to share. He glanced at his communications device and pushing a few buttons, located her at the astrometry laboratory. He changes directions and walked towards her location.

Within a few minutes he was inside looking for her. He received directions and found his way to a back secluded lab. This one had multiple displays, some holographic, that depicted their position in the solar system, local star field and where Earth was in relation to the new planet.

"Excuse me, Camomile?"

"Yes? Hello Stephen, how are you?"

"Doing well, Thank you. And you?"

"Quite well, busy of course. What brings you to my lab?"

"As you know, I am preparing a report for the people back on Earth. I have talked with quite a few people here and am getting a general sense that this is great place to live. However there are some realities that we did not expect to find and maybe even some behaviors we were not predicting, like the Commander and the Android."

"Yes, I know. I think we are finding that these events are possibly connected. The satellite and mother

287

ship telescopes have found some interesting things."

"Do you have time to discuss these?"

"I have some time, we are scheduled for another observing run in an hour. We have to prepare and calibrate which will take a few minutes beforehand."

"Okay, we can be quick. Then I have some other business to attend to in town."

"Okay, perfect. Let's sit down."

They found a place around a lab bench and sat down in technician's chairs.

Camomile pointed a device towards a screen on the wall, pushed a button and spoke first.

"Here is our planet, I have highlighted our village. As I zoom in and move around, you see that it looks like the paradise that it is. Then, if I place a marker where the Commander landed you see that it is in fact as far away from the village as you could get; I don't think he wants contact with us anymore. Then watch as I place markers on the known positions of the Android, Frank. You see them leaving the village as soon as he arrived, then as he moved about we can extrapolate his path. Notice that upon arrival he went out pretty far, maybe wandered and explored a bit, stayed in one area for a while then returned to find (and probably observe) us from a vantage point that provided a view of the whole village. Once the Commander landed however, Frank left immediately and is now moving directly towards the landing point of the Commander's shuttle. All of this is interesting however we notice that Frank chose a route through a very particular area of the forrest. Notice that he slowed down here, both times in fact. Once when he was exploring and now just as he moved through that area again. So now, look as we zoom in to this area. We have used hyper spectral imaging to filter out the vegetation. Do you see the structures underneath? More filtering an enhancement from multiple look angles give us an even clearer picture. These structures are in perfect condition, geometrically shaped and positioned along the magnetic field lines of the planet. Also, we think that some of the faces, corners and other openings point towards important locations in the sky at certain times of the year. On Earth there were multiple structures designed this way, Stonehenge, Medicine Wheel, the Pyramids etc. The structures on this planet are similar but a much more modern look. The angles of the walls and roof line are very exact. These were well thought out structures.

Now lets look at something else, here I will overlay some of our readings in the ultraviolet, magnetic, gamma ray and x-ray regions of the electromagnetic spectrum. You see the pulsations? They are precisely the same length of time, peak to peak as a fraction of the time this planet circles the sun. We don't know if it's a resonance or purposefully designed but we can tell you that there is a lot of energy down there."

"Wow, that is amazing. I have to say though that the scientific data you have revealed is probably part of a greater story here."

"What do you mean?"

"Martin for instance, has been sensing some kind of energy in space. He has morphed, maybe even evolved into another sub-species of human being. He does not look like us anymore and cannot live in our level of gravity. Most likely he will live out the rest of his life with the stars. He talked about having an epiphany, sensing things that were hard to put into words. He felt that something was definitely going on with this planet and the environment around it. And then there is Peg. She senses that something is going on with the animals, I actually witnessed it, they are somehow communicating with something, themselves or something external. I can't tell. When Buck died, they formed geometric patterns around his burial spot."

"Well I have heard other rumors as well, and I think we certainly have to explore the area with the buildings, my guess is that there are some answers there."

"Yes I agree. For now though I think I will go back to the village to get dinner. Thank you for your time Camomile. Let me know if I can help."

"Your welcome, Stephen. And yes, I think you of all people should go and see this place. We will need the experience documented. From what we can tell, there is a lot going on there."

With that, Stephen smiled at her, rose and left the laboratory. She spun back around in her chair and continued her explorations. She had a very serious side to her, once engaged with an interesting task, she would be relentless until she finished it.

He left the science building and went back outside to find his way back to the food area. "Now things were getting interesting," he thought. He decided to have dinner, review his notes on the stories he had been told and start to compile an outline for the report to Earth. The sun was going down and the temperature was getting very pleasant. Maybe he would eat outside.

The commissary was active when he arrived. Lots of people talking and sitting at tables. He went in and found a place to sit. Of course, he hoped his favorite waitress would be there so he could say hello. She was, he found out, but taking care of another section of the eatery. Another waiter instead took his order. As he sat, he pulled out his electronic note pad and started to draft an outline. So many things had transpired this day that he needed to organize his thoughts. Soon his food appeared and he both ate and typed. By the time he finished he had produced several pages of notes that would help him produce a decent report. He was taking his final sips of tea when he was interrupted.

"Hey."

Stephen looked up to see his favorite waitress, smiled a genuine smile and said:

"Hey! Hello Leah, how are you?"

"Doing well. What was your name?"

"Stephen, Stephen Daedalus."

"Well, Stephen, Stephen Daedalus, my shift is over in a few minutes. Would you like to go get some coffee?"

"Absolutely, Leah. I would love to. Shall I meet you outside?"

"Sure, it will be about fifteen minutes if that is okay."

"No problem. I will find a place to sit outside and just continue my work.'

"Okay, see you then!"

Stephen had a glowing feeling going on and he

quickly finished what he was doing, organized his dishes, got up and left.

It was even cooler outside now and the stars were just beginning to appear. He found a bench, sat down and reviewed his writings of the last hour, although he was really not able to concentrate.

Leah showed up about twenty minutes later and sat down beside him.

"What are you working on?"

"Oh, this is the draft outline of a report I am writing on how we have adapted to our new planet. Earth wants to know if there are any dangers or concerns."

He looked up at her and continued.

"What do you think?"

She thought for a few moments and said:

"This place is wonderful. It was easy to adapt to, get use to the climate and start living. To be honest with you, I do not miss Earth at all, with the exception of family and friends. We talk as much as we can over the communication channels but I really do not want to leave this place. It has a serenity that is intoxicating. I get up every morning in a good mood, looking forward to going to work or just exploring on my days off. Everyone here seems relaxed as well. On Earth, I came from a pretty depressing area of the U.S. where poverty and disease was taking over. There were too many people and the separation of haves and have nots was overwhelming. The rich lived in palaces and we lived in shacks. I was so happy to get out of there and find hope on another planet.

So to answer your question, there are always dangers and concerns in a new place. That is normal and we must work together to persevere. We did it many times on Earth as people explored new continents and the wilderness. I think our greatest challenge will be to make sure we do not ignore history and doom ourselves to repeat it."

Stephen let the words sink in a bit and replied:

"Yes your right, this is a wonderful place and I agree that we should be careful in how we exist here. We cannot just exploit the area and leave waste. We know better. Also I think we are going to have to control our population. We did not do that effectively on Earth and it exploded. The consequences were food shortages, pollution and wars."

"Yes, we need to avoid that mistake."

There was silence for several seconds as each was thinking about what to say next. Leah spoke first.

"For now, how about a walk and maybe some coffee?"

"Perfect."

They rose, chose a direction and started to walk slowly. A coffee shop was reasonably close and they headed in that general direction.

As they walked, they spoke of several people they knew in common and generally got to know each. They would become friends.

Maria's coffee shop was nearby, within a minute or two there were at the front door and went in. It was air conditioned and smelled of coffee, tea and lavender. Maria was one of the people on the mother ship assigned to feed the others. She could make dinner for hundreds of people or make coffee for a couple. Tonight she did the latter. She greeted them from across the counter.

"Hello Leah, Stephen, how are you guys this evening?"

"Doing great, just taking a walk and talking."

"Glad to see that, ha! You're a cute couple."

"Well thank you, Maria. We're just getting to know each," Stephen said. "And, I am kind of interviewing most everyone here for a report I need to send back to Earth."

"Well, if you want my opinion, I love this place."

"Most everyone does."

"Especially since the Commander is not here."

"Yes, it seems everyone agrees with that as well. So, any other thoughts or feelings?"

"Well, not so much. I work quite a bit now, if it's not the coffee shop it the home stuff. Every once in a while, I get to stop and consider what we have done, where we are from and what we are going to do here in the future. I assume we are staying, no one seems to think otherwise."

"No, they don't."

"So sometimes when I have time off, I like to go hiking. I feel incredibly comfortable out in the woods. This place has vibes, good vibes."

"Many of us feel that vibe, several of us have actually looking into what it really might be. Would you be concerned if we end up finding out that this place has other sentient life forms?"

"No, of course not, especially if they are friendly."

"I suspect they are."

"Oh, sounds like there is a lot going on with the scientists."

"Yes and also the people that interact with animals."

"Peg for instance?"

"Yes."

"Well, I like Peg and trust her. If she says something is going on you need to listen."

"I did, and I do. Her animals have shown some unusual behavior, not bad or dangerous, just a bit unusual."

"How so?"

"They sometimes synchronize their movements."

"Oh, I think I have seen some of that out in the woods. Not all of the time but every once in a while you see animals lining up or all looking one way, things like that. It's just different from Earth behavior. Probably the strangest thing I witnessed was predator and prey doing the same thing, without regard to their positions in the animal kingdom. It's a little magical."

Leah chimed in, "Yes, sometimes it is a little magical around here. The plants are different but good, the animals are different but good. Every once in a while when I am outside at night, I see a very faint line in the sky, it seems to follow our equator. Have you seen this, Stephen?"

"Yes I have, from the mother ship. It is a faint ring of ice particles, just like Saturn's. With the right angle to the sun, it changes colors. The astronomers are trying to discover what it is made of. Right not they think it is ice, much like Saturn's"

Maria remembered why they were in her shop.

"Coffee?"

"Yes, two cups. Mine with a little milk. Leah?"

"Just sugar for me, thanks."

"Okay, just give me a few minutes, go and sit down and I will bring them to you."

"Ok, thanks Maria."

Stephen and Leah, turned from the counter, found a table near the window and sat down. Stephen sat back to think about what was next with the new phenomena, Leah watched him for a second and then felt comfortable that she was out, talking to someone interesting and part of a happy group of people.

Their drinks came within a few minutes and after thanking Maria, went about sipping and enjoying their coffee. Stephen stopped pondering and offered some concluding remarks.

"I think we need to go explore the structures in the forrest."

"Yes, I agree, it seems to be a big part of this story. We need to understand it before we make our final decision to stay."

"Yep."

A few more minutes passed in silence as they worked on their coffees.

Then Stephen spoke.

"I am going to talk to several people I know and ask

them to go with me to the ruins."

"Who are you thinking about taking?"

"Camomile, Rudy, Peg, I will put Martin on a radio link and you if you are interested."

"Of course, I would love to see the ruins and find out what is going on."

"Ok, then. I will contact them tonight on email, then let you know what the schedule is."

"Great!"

They sat in silence for a few moments longer then started to talk about other things, just to keep the conversation going.

In about 30 minutes, they were finished. After cleaning up their cups and plates, they rose, said goodbye to Maria and headed for the door.

Stephen walked her back to the food area and while doing that she asked:

"Do you know Leah Smith?"

"Yes, she was my great grandmother."

"Mine too."

"Huh. What made you think of that?"

"I'm not sure, but you look like my Dad and so I had to ask."

"Thats amazing, I don't know much about that side

of the family. If I remember correctly, they got very religious and drifted away."

"Yes, they did, in fact it got very weird. I had to leave at an early age as they were putting a lot of pressure on me to marry an older man who was a deacon at the church."

"So you escaped?"

"I did, in fact I got a scholarship to go to college, fell off of their radar screens and applied to go on this trip. The rest is history as they say."

Stephen smiled broadly. "So we are related."

"Yes indeed, we are blood, which is good because you are not my type."

"What? I'm crushed! I thought we were going to hit it off and have a good time together."

"We will I'm sure. And I am looking forward to it."

"Me too. So what is your type?"

"Silent."

"Well that is not me."

Stephen smiled again and felt good about having a new friend but maybe a bit saddened that there was no future otherwise. "So be it," he thought. He returned to the present world.

"I will contact everyone I mentioned and let you

know when we are going to meet up."

"Ok, thanks Stephen."

They were now where they had started, she gave him a peck on the cheek and went inside. He watched her go, smiled and then made his way back to his quarters.

The Nietzchans

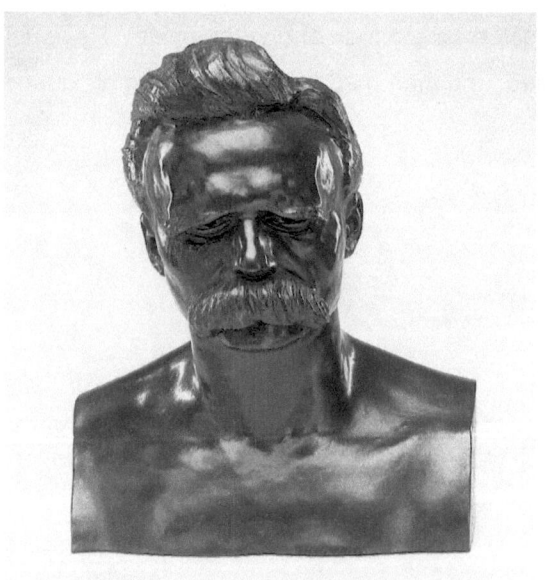

"Madness is something rare in individuals – but in groups, parties, peoples and ages, it is rule." - Friedrich Nietzsche

Stephen coordinated with the others to do an exploratory trip to where they found the buildings. He worked with the Mother Ship to get the latest satellite imagery, the latest position of Frank and the latest known position of the Commander.

Interestingly, the day before they set out, Frank changed his direction of travel and started on a return path to the buildings. Stephen and the others were informed about this change and knew that they would probably meet Frank there.

The morning came for the departure, Rudy, Camomile, Peg, Leah and Stephen met at the edge of the village and set off following the path that Frank had taken. They brought enough food and water for several days as well as scientific equipment they thought would be useful.

They were on their way by 7 am and were over half way to their destination by noon. They stopped for lunch and a short examination of the surroundings. The plants and animals seems about the same as near the village. It was still idyllic with fresh air and the smells of exotic flowers. Birds were about making noise and as they had moved from area to area during the morning walk, they could tell they were leaving small habitats occupied by groups of animals.

After lunch and a bit of research, they set off again for the buildings. It was calculated that they would reach them by late afternoon. Hopefully if all went well, they would stay overnight and return the next day.

While they walked they had comm links to the village via the Mother Ship. Their progress was being mapped at both places as well. Just in case of trouble, another pilot was standing by in the Village ready to retrieve them with a tilt rotor aircraft.

The day became warm and as they progressed they took breaks every hour or so. The local stream water checked out well and they drank as needed, sometimes soaking their hats or shirts in the water to keep cool.

At some point they realized that they were less than an hour away. They stopped to take their final break before the last push and sat amongst the vegetation. Although still hot, there was a breeze which felt good. They drank fluids and had small snacks.

As they sat and quietly talked amongst themselves, one of realized the environment was different.

"Do you hear that?"

"Hear what," asked Stephen

"Silence."

"Hmmm, you're right. It is very quiet here, even the wind is quiet. And look at how the branches and leaves move, as if in slow motion."

"Yeah, it's a little weird. My instruments say

everything is okay however my chronometer seems to be running much quicker."

Stephen checked his watch and followed the second hand for a while.

"You're right, my watch is moving very quickly. I feel fine but this day is moving quickly. We should probably get to our destination before it gets dark."

They rose and got everybody's attention. All of them were now experiencing this time dilation. It was very similar to how they lived on the Mother Ship. They took drugs to slow down their metabolism which rendered the effect of fast moving clocks. To each person, all was well, but the world was moving a lot quicker.

They started off again towards the buildings and the effect became more pronounced. As a result they started to hurry and walk faster. The sun was definitely moving in the sky as they saw their destination a few hundred meters away and by this time they were almost running to keep up with the day. Soon, they arrived, breathing hard and sweating. The sun went down hours before they were expecting it to, however they found that the building actually glowed a bit allowing them to see.

During their final fast walk (if not run), animals were following them and plants seemed to be moving to face their flowers at them as they went by. All of this made them a bit nervous and made them move a bit faster.

Once in the building compound they sat down and caught their breath. It took a few minutes, diluted minutes, before they felt strong enough to consider their surroundings. The ones who had scientific instruments started making measurements immediately. Others started looking around and trying to understand the structures.

"These walls are perfectly smooth."

"And perfectly aligned with the magnetic lines of force."

"The time dilation effect seems strongest here, we might be staying here for a while compared to village time."

It was definitely dark now, the stars were visible and you could detect their subtle movement. They relaxed and ate dinner then decided to look around the buildings some more. They had a general feeling that they should not stay very long, especially with the time dilation phenomena. People at home would be getting nervous by now. Then someone realized that they had not heard anything from the Mother Ship.

"The comms are out, they seem to be way off frequency."

"Makes sense, even their internal oscillators are

moving up in frequency."

"Or our speech is so low that it does not make sense."

"Could be, in any event we should not spend too much time here, no pun intended."

"Agreed."

At that moment they saw a figure approaching them from the forrest trail. They gathered together instinctively for protection. The figure drew closer and at some point someone realized who it was."

"Frank?"

There was no reply initially, but it came closer, clearly in view and stopped.

"Greetings everyone."

"Frank! How are you?"

"Doing well, but we need to leave immediately and go somewhere to talk."

"Why Frank?"

"Because the closer you get to the heart of this building area, the more time dilation you will experience and at some point you will not be visible or able to communicate with the others."

Stephen saw the reasoning in this statement, the others were quickly getting there as well.

"Ok Frank, lead the way."

They gathered their instruments and other belongings and followed Frank, somewhat quickly and directly away from the structures. The walk took thirty minutes, after which they were basically exhausted. Frank finally stopped, the rest collapsed behind him and most reached for water bottles.

"You are safe here," Frank said in a monotone voice, not his usual human, caring voice.

"What's going on back there?" Stephen asked.

"There is another race, a very advanced race, which is present in those buildings. They use and create a significant amount of energy which causes a gravity well, much like a very small black hole. Time is dilated significantly while you are close to those buildings. It is important that we do not stay in that area for a long period of time as we could be sent well into the future."

"Okay, understood. So can you tell us more about this civilization?"

"Yes, they call themselves the Neitzchans. They knew you were coming and they know everything you are doing. You are welcome here, the Commander is not and has been dealt with."

"How so?" asked Camomile.

"They knew his personality was a clash with their moral principles and they influenced him to leave the ship and take up residence on the far side of the planet. The animals will take care of him there."

"What are you saying? They are going to eat him."

"No, the animals there are far more intelligent than him, they will calm him down and let him live his life out. If you ever see him again you will not recognize him. Right now his memory is full of his abuses and he is too embarrassed to contact you. You should leave him alone for a few years."

"I don't think that will be a problem. He alienated everyone, took what he could and let us know that he was superior to all of us. It was a waste of energy, the voyage could have been farm more enjoyable and productive without his disruptions."

Frank continued. "I witnessed quite a bit of stress on the voyage, much more than what was expected. According to psychological data in the archives he would have been diagnosed with paranoia and an over inflated ego."

"Ultimately we think he was afraid and he took it out on us. We did the work and he was very critical of our activities and general manner. We are however, a space faring civilization and professionals. We knew what we were getting into, dealt properly with whatever fears and concern we had, and did our jobs."

"I agree, but now you are in a new world. I have explored about 1% of it and it is, in your terms, wondrous."

By now the group had settled down from their vigorous walk. All were watching Frank intently, they had many questions but in general felt it was good to have him back.

Rudy asked the next question.

"Frank, I have been flying around this area recently, both in my plane as well as using a drone. We see the building site most of the time and have been watching it. Are there more building sites around the planet?"

"Yes, there are. Some you will discover, many you will not. The Nietzchans are far advanced from us and can live in multiple dimensions. They are with us now but at some point you will discover that the building site we just left is no longer there. It is here because they are interested in us. They tell me that we have much to offer and represent some of the best features of their past. We are, in their minds, good people and have the aptitude for discovery and growth. Their civilization is defined by these attributes. They tell me that it will be difficult for us to understand what they now understand, but they assure us that we are on the right path.

The future is the overwhelming focus of these beings and they teach that each thing we as sentient beings do, completely drive the future. We have to define what we want and take all of the steps, no matter how small, towards that or those goals."

"That's good to hear. So they won't eat us?"

"They do not have mouths."

"Good to hear, then how maintain themselves? Are they just computer programs?"

"No, far beyond that. They maintain themselves by converting energy. When humans eat, they do the same as well as provide water and nutrients to their biological systems. The Nietzchans occupy space, can appear anywhere in our local star system, and can exist without form. They are the result of integration of body and machine. This was the first step of many for them. Energy is the key ingredient so considering that mass is energy according to Einstein, they reside in or near mass."

"So Einstein was right?"

"Absolutely, but he only scratched the surface. With access to all available knowledge, a perfect memory and extremely fast thinking skills the next Einsteins will accelerate us to the future. The Nietzchans tell me that those next Einsteins will be your progeny."

Camomile asked the next question.

"Frank, will you come back and stay with us?"

"Yes, always. I am to be your guide as well as assistant."

"Thank you, good to hear."

Camomile asked:

"Frank, are they able to explore the cosmos with telescopes and similar instruments?"

"Absolutely, and if they were ever to have a religion it would be based on cosmic discovery. As you know there are an enormous amount of discoveries waiting out there for us. The Nietzchans tell me that we are vastly underestimating the total amount. In fact, are far from understanding the best questions to ask. They tell me we will get there someday and to be patient. For now they insist we build our telescopes and measuring instruments and appreciate every thing they tell us."

"Good to hear, you mentioned religion, where is that headed for us?"

"At some point you will realize that animism which led to pantheism then polytheism then monotheism were really a reflection of the human's definition of self. God as it turns out, is us. In many people there is a predilection for religious or spiritual feelings, these are here for many reasons and similar feelings pervade the Galaxy. It is one of the things that most sentient beings have in common. It guides many and sets the moral compass and defines the mores for decent behavior. All of this is good. The Nietzchans understand this and find that it gives comfort for those who need it and it gives direction as well."

"So, is there a future for religion?"

"Yes, but not in its present form. Too many people back on Earth defined it for their own good. Few people there try to understand the common denominators between all of the religions and as a result, millions of people lost their lives to subset beliefs. All of that is gone in the future and replaced by an integrated consciousness that combines all of the attributes of life and thought. There is more harmony to look forward to. The disagreements and discontents of modern civilization will long be forgotten as they are a waste of time. And time is the ultimate non-reusable resource."

Peg asked the last question.

"Will we be able to communicate or interact with the Nietzchans?"

"You are right now. At some point they will invite us

back here to give us a more corporeal display and an opportunity to get to know them better. For now they ask that we settle in and enjoy life on this planet."

With that, they looked at each other, then Frank and collectively thought it was time to leave and go home. Frank came with them and answered questions about the flora and fauna he had discovered. Some of the geology he said, "was amazing" as this planet was made up of a slightly different set of ingredients as Earth. He told them that they would have decades of discovery for both themselves and their children.

Within a few hours, they had returned, the others who had been following their progress greeted Frank warmly and within a few hours, life returned to normal. There was work to be done to keep this village viable as well as vibrant.

Report to those on Earth

       Several days after their encounter with the Nietzchans, Stephen sat down to write the report that was to be sent back home to Earth. It is reproduced in the following pages:

Report to NASA Space Council, ESA and the International Space Consortium

S. Daedalus

Dear Distinguished Friends and Colleagues,

The following is a report on the voyage, landing and colonization of astronaut group 101A in the interstellar ship Gaea to the Planet 4E of the Trappist 1 system.

Detailed archives have been telemetered about the moment by moment details of the voyage and subsequent operations to Earth from the launch until the present day. This is a synopsis of the events that occurred and is intended to serve only as an overview.

A carefully vetted list of astronauts were picked from candidates who represented many cultures from Earth. They are scientists engineers, pilots, agronomists and animal specialists. They flew a successful mission, taking several years using hibernation techniques, self sustaining biospheres and good piloting. In general the voyage was uneventful, save for some global concerns from the crew about the Commander's management style. Interviews with the crew indicated that they were all made to feel uncomfortable at some point during the journey. Many who had close contact with the Commander spoke of high levels of stress and fatigue as a result of his command style. Asked to describe the most challenging part of their voyage, each crew member cited the Commander. Subsequent to landing, the Commander sequestered himself and eventually loaded his personal belongings onto the Commander's shuttle and flew down to the planet's surface. During this trip, he purposefully turned off any electronic equipment designed to allow him to be tracked. Radar and other sensory equipment onboard the mother ship was able to follow his progress however and it was discovered that he flew to the antipodal point from the established village. He did not communicate his intentions to the remaining crew nor to anyone on the surface and has not been heard of since. We surmise that he wanted to leave the group, retire and hopefully deal with a memory full of his abuses.

The village, now called "Gentuu" is functioning well. All of the primary human habitability systems are in place and operating properly. Energy is supplied by wind and solar and is distributed via fiber optics. We have reliable communications throughout the village area and around the planet via microsats. Water is plentiful as is food. Most of our food is made from 3D printers but we are slowly getting used to the vegetation surround the village and how to cook it.

This planet has most of the same geological issues that Earth does, with minor earthquakes, similar chemical makeup and a combination of mountains and lowlands. It is roughly the size of Earth and has several small moons situated within a fine ring structure situated on the equatorial plane. The ring is mostly ice and at certain times around dawn and dusk, can be seen projected in the sky.

From an environmental point of view, this planet has the air, water and land quality of Earth a thousand years ago. There is no evidence of pollution or any other type of environmental abuse. The result of living here is clearer minds, less disease and longer life. The medical staff here are astonished at how well the human body functions on this planet. The cancer rates have diminished to zero and the lower carbon dioxide rates have allowed increased oxygen levels to prevent heart disease and increase mental performance.

The societal structure is harmonious with large decisions made by all and lower level decisions made by appointed representatives. All discussion, laws and proposed legislation are available through multiple information outlets with everyone allowed to comment.

The issue of money is non-existent. Once it was

determined that accumulating wealth was a waste of time, people found they were no longer interested in symbols of financial success.

All in all, the society here is stable, happy and has adapted well to the new surroundings.

The only issue or concern is the discovery of an ancient / advanced civilization on the planet's surface. The first pieces of evidence about this civilization came from the high resolution images from space, followed by low elevation images from drones. The android, Frank had first contact with it soon thereafter and discovered that what appeared to be ruins were actually very modern building using materials and techniques we are not familiar with.

An expedition was mounted by some of our members to get a better look at the area. I was part of this group and as we got closer we experienced significant time dilation and other physical effects. Our relative time, that amongst the group seemed to be proper however all of our chronometers, the sun and other physical phenomena, were moving much faster. As we reached the buildings we were met by Frank, who was waiting for us. He quickly led us directly away from the structures and once we were at a safe distance stopped and explained what we were experiencing. He knows quite a bit about these structures and the people who built them. He assures us we are safe but we must keep clear of the buildings or we could experience long lasting time transport. In other words, someone who purposefully spends time there could come back to our village one hundred years from now if they are not careful.

That being said, Frank advises us that these people are clearly aware of our presence and welcome us to their world. He says they pose no threat but need us to respect their privacy. He also believes that in the future, they will initiate a dialogue with us. They wish us to know them and to understand who they are.

They call themselves the Nietzchans and, according to Frank, are millions of years older that us. At present they do not have a corporeal existence but can if they wish. They exist using significant amounts of electro magnetic energy which explains the time warping as it is created by a very small black hole. The energy they have access to and there non corporeal existence allows them to exist in many places at once, including places that are very far away. They take advantage of the quantum entanglement properties and time dilation to explore vast areas of space. Their intelligence is vast and encompasses the thoughts, experiences and knowledge of all of their people as well as all that have come before them. They have assimilated computer capabilities and several other scientific advancements we have yet to learn. According to Frank, they do not want to put us in shock but would like to live peacefully by us. We are all in agreement and in some ways feel safer with them than without.

This brings me to the another phenomena that we have experienced here on this planet. It is one we cannot fully explain at this time but we think it might be related to the current inhabitants.

The animals, including the ones we brought, exhibit unique behavior at times. They seem to synchronize their attention on one subject and can form shapes by standing in particular areas. We had a loss during the first few months after our arrival. Our lead animal specialist had a heart attack and passed away out in a large pasture. It look a long time before anyone found him but during that time a multitude of animals gathered around him and started forming geometric shapes and moving in synchrony. A passer by finally noticed the animal behavior and called the medical team to come help. Of course it was too late but the interesting thing was that the animals had formed concentric circles around the body. The first circle was composed of horses, the second of cows, then other species followed. Predator and prey animals stood next to each other without fear or concern. To the people who found the body, the animals somehow conveyed that they wanted the body to be buried in place as a memorial. This was done and a mound was also built above with a large tree in the center. The animals still inspect it every once in a while but have not formed the geometric figures.

This phenomena has happened a few more times, not as a result of a death but for other reasons. It was noted during the exploration of the buildings that the local animals exhibited odd behavior especially when they got closer to the structures. Some of the scientist here also believe that the plant life is responding in synchrony as well.

At this point we can only tell you that these events are happening, that we see no danger in it and that again we believe that the interesting behavior of flora and fauna is somehow connected to the actions of the indigenous people here.

In conclusion, we were safely transported here and have found a comfortable place to inhabit. The environment is clean and hospitable and we see no reason for concern. Our lives have adjusted to the new surroundings and all of us consider this home now.

Epilogue

Twenty two years later a second ship arrived from Earth. It was essentially the same design and crew compliment. As Earth had sent several ships to various planets to find new places to live, they discovered after Stephen's first and subsequent reports, that this planet was one of the best choices. If the second ship corroborated his observations, then more would come.

Once the ship entered orbit, it began the process of locating the first ship. It was discovered that there was a single person on board who made no attempt to contact the new arrivals. A shuttle was sent over to meet him and once he was found it was discovered that he had morphed into a non-human state and was incapable of living in any sort of gravity. His body had lengthened by almost a meter and his head was significantly enlarged.

Martin was his name and he found it difficult to communicate with the crew members of the new ship. At some point during the discussions, he asked to be left alone and the crew members granted his request.

Other crew members were sent down to the surface. It should be mentioned here that while enroute the second ship lost communications with the original ship's crew members. All telemetry ceased and any sign of activity disappeared.

When the landing party found their way into the village named Gentuu, they found it completely abandoned and somewhat changed physically. It was completely cleaned up with all of any perishable foods missing. All of the quarters were in pristine shape as were the offices and laboratories. All electricity was shut off but interestingly, the monitors on the many computer systems glowed a pale blue. The walls and ceilings seemed to glow a bit as well.

Once more scientists and technicians came down to explore the village it was found that a small amount of time dilation was occurring, somewhat like what Stephen Daedalus had described in his report. The magnitude was low but the effect was real. It was decided not to spend too much time in the Village for the same reason that the report had warned about with the other structures on the planet.

Before leaving the village, a scientist was able to activate and down load some of Stephen's last notes.

The original villages had started to interact with the Nietzchans. Somehow they felt comfortable in doing so and started spending more and more time at the ancient structures several miles away from the village.

Stephen's final entry in his journal was:

"The only way to see the future is to go there."

ABOUT THE AUTHOR

Kevin Shoemaker was born in New York City in April of 1954. A son of an actress and musician turned professor. He has lived in several states and has been educated in the fields of philosophy, radio astronomy and antenna design. He has authored several technical papers in astronomy and has many patents in the fields of aviation, antenna design, radar and meteorology. In addition, he is an avid pilot and boat owner and holds several certificates for operating airplanes, helicopters, performing flight instruction and is a licensed Captain in the Merchant Marines. Currently he works as an antenna and radar designer near Cape Canaveral. Mr. Shoemaker is a father of one daughter and one son and lives in Indian Harbour Beach.

Comments? e-mail: Shoemakerlabs@gmail.com

Other books by the author:

Mars Life

Practical Antenna Design

The Voyages of Gaea

Sunrise Descending

Life in the Universe and Where to Find It

Views from the Balcony

Pluto Dreams of Persephone

Practical Antenna Design - 1st and 2nd Editions